RAMONA

N. BALAJI

INDIA • SINGAPORE • MALAYSIA

ISBN
Paperback 979-8-89610-724-8
Hardcase 979-8-89777-396-1

CONTENTS

Acknowledgment	5
Ramona and her Social Rise	7
Memoirs De Voyageurs	13
Three 'P's - (1) Perspiration	34
(2) Persistence	40
Brian with his Sweet Heart	75
Children's School Education	90
Tenth Wedding Anniversary	92
Natasha's School Picnic	96
Public Service & Political Involvement	102
Brian And Jonas Nathan Encounter	107
An Ode to Zurich	125
Birth Of a New Political Party	132
Mother's Lessons to Natasha and Ambrose	135
Caroline, Ramona's Best Friend!	139
Caroline's Induction	141
Nomination for Election	145
Election Campaign	147
Nathan's Game of Politics	150

Strategic Campaign & Election Violence ... 152

Peoples' Verdict ... 157

Nathan's Revenge ... 158

Brian's Personal Loss ... 160

Ramona's Final Journey ... 163

Brian's Lunatic Swings ... 166

Police Action ... 168

(3) Prize: Brian's Ascendancy ... 169

Court Scenes ... 176

Brian's Return ... 179

Loyalty - Live On Your Ambition Limited To Yourself! ... 183

Epilogue ... *185*

ACKNOWLEDGMENT

Notably, during the challenging moments I faced, it was the unwavering support of my close relatives, especially my wife, Mrs Rama, as well as both children, Arti and Amar, besides a few dependable friends, that truly stood out. Their constant presence and encouragement served as a guiding light, steering me through the difficulties that came my way. Without their reassuring words and comforting presence, the task at hand would have become insurmountable, almost like a mirage in the desert, appearing real yet unattainable.

In today's world, the phrase "Thank you" has unfortunately lost much of its sincere meaning due to overuse in commercial contexts. The genuine sentiment of gratitude has been overshadowed by its oft-repeat superficial usage.

In light of this unfortunate trend, I feel compelled to express my appreciation in a more profound manner. Therefore, I extend my gratitude to each and every individual who has supported me, not just as a group, but also on a personal level.

My cordial "Namaste" goes out to those who have been there for me, showing me kindness and understanding in times of need.

RAMONA AND HER SOCIAL RISE

"Ramona, why have you brought these eggs and bread packets without selling them in the market? Why did you come home so early?" It was Ramona's mother, with her slovenly and faded but typically rustic clothes, chastising Ramona. "No, Mom, I was hungry and tired. I came home to get some bites from you and then I will go to the market again for selling," Ramona's soft voice flowed.

"OK, don't take too long in that job," her mother said. "We have more work to do." Saying so, her mother gave her some bread loaves. "Come fast, and we need to go to the farmlands of Uncle Dias to pluck the maize crops. Then, we will have to take the truckload to the warehouse for unloading before sunset."

For a tender girl of 7 years, the work schedule was grueling. More often, the body pain made her cry, sitting on the mud road for hours together, and when her mother rushed to locate her missing daughter, she got up to pursue her work. Her early childhood life as a helper in farmlands, a packing girl in meat and food courts, and a helper in electrical and plastic retail shops, was a drudgery world that would collapse the adult laborers of their early budding life. Moreover, cleaning classrooms after school hours and at different jobs and different levels entailed a serious risk to personal safety as hooligans and exploitative elements trolled her to comply with their personal favors.

Born as the last baby in a large, neglected, poverty-stricken family, Ramona cried, desired and agitated for all of her baby needs, yet unsympathetically was punished out of sheer economic affordability even when she was just a tender child. Every child undergoes such apathy in their household, even in today's rural, urban and most developed country sites without exception. Some elite households too witness this trend! Such traumatic experiences indelibly rubbed a wound and Ramona, inclusive.

This early childhood unusually generated a sympathetic view of her brethren laborers. She grew up to share her helping tendency with others in farm and market areas. Normally, the child market labor exploited and enslaved the growing years of a tender child, devoid of hope and pushing her to adopt conniving and a negative social role, yet Ramona was a positive exception in her later years!

The law and police, with some formidable social institutions for child development and welfare, cast their eagle eyes and help only a few victims return to their lives. A small solace, our social systems are working. In that ordeal, some hapless children succumb tragically.

Ramona in anomalous and precarious situations was threatened with her constant survival that pushed her to learn all the lessons of surpassing the inhumane circumstances on her own and upgrade herself to expertly wade through life's tentacles.

Once in her job in a plastic and nylon fashion mart, the poor small girl asked for payment from a haughty customer for her purchases and the customer freely swinging her ID 'Clara' around her neck demanded, "Pack up these nylon bands and scarves. Hurry up and give the balance, I've got to rush now", without paying for the purchase. The customer demanded the physical check of Ramona by her sales colleagues in the presence of the franchise owner. Stuck by her intensity of innocence, Ramona brought the customer's deceitful trait to the fore. Still, for a small defenseless girl to go through such humiliation in the presence of a public gathering, who was, in the end, labeled a petty 'thief', it was a shocking experience and a harakiri for Ramona.

The mental trauma impacted by this episode forced her to quit her job despite her boss's insistence not to do so and seek shelter elsewhere in a fresh locale, in a fit of urgency to uphold her personal dignity.

Often society fails to impose its finest character of responsibility to protect the hapless and defenseless people from injustice and bring mischief mongers to justice as it fears the widespread repercussions of its corrective actions. This tendency, while bolstering undue social activities, contributes by all means to the misery of working girls, as a timid class that buckles.

She then resolved mentally that if ever she got a chance in the future, she would bring all her folks together as a team under one umbrella that would engage primarily to teach and cultivate various livelihood vocations and then, unitedly stand against the suppressive forces.

That she was to play a larger role in the general development of women as a constructive team to build and attune their economic security in the plight of their vulnerable defense in society was a foresight that made miracles a current reality!

In building the social mixture of a subsistence economy to help womenfolk eke out their livelihood, she encountered threats from well-established entrepreneurs, higher-echelon peers of both genders to forsake her enterprising efforts and, in extreme situations, tactics deployed to maim her life! She miraculously escaped with scathing injuries, jabbed punctures, or minor brushes, spreading continuous jitters among her rivals. The contract killers adorned in civilian garb were still roaming, with guns, daggers and machetes hidden in their jackets to knife her passively.

Since all women went through similar experiences, their understanding of the societal position and knowledge of their living conditions, she trained them to become an army of sorts. Their aim was to protect themselves from such social and religious oppressive forces and intimidatory tactics solely to guard their survival.

With clarity of purpose edged in her mind, she determined to start on an experimental basis to organize a group of women for discussion or tête-à-tête and invited all women to assemble at the auditorium of the town's school, that Sunday evening at 3.00 p.m.

The assemblage thronged even outside the auditorium and witnessing such a large gathering at the very first clarion, Ramona felt numbed to realize if all that gathering was a bona fide credential of their suffering. An iron lady she was, she was determined to stand by them all of her life! Segregated the assemblage on the basis of their proximate residence and ability to meet and instantly support one another to avert crises, she addressed them in her low modulation, "We have gathered here to earn our dignity and our right to a peaceful life. It was not the Divine Law that subjected us to suffer and to cater to the whims of our fellow gents. Whenever you were subjected to such humiliation or were witnessing elsewhere, you got to rise yourself and with your other member volunteers, bring such perpetrators to their senses. We all stand in unity, come what may."

She amassed all womenfolk at the open arena and group-wise split to take different vocations like arts such as painting, and crafts like toy making, baby care products, artificial jewelry, fashion emporium, and in scores of unimaginable areas to hone their talents. For all such activities, she, as their leader, advocated for financial support from various social institutions, and they all succeeded largely by pooling internal funds to meet exigencies.

The social participation coupled with lavish moral support from her team gradually brought their achievements to the limelight! Until then, people and large corporate bodies declined to identify them, looking elsewhere, but now took a swift turn to recognize their might and patronize them, chiefly to boost their selfish growth, in and as part of their own business strategy!

Taking a studious assessment of their involvement and growth, Ramona just made a mental note to bring all their corporals into the union to support her husband Brian's public policy and to polarize the voter public in his favor.

MEMOIRS DE VOYAGEURS

In one of the remote railway stations, where the name plate of the town read as Neigay, a tall and thin bespectacled man in baggy blue trousers, a loose shirt with its collar flipping on his left shoulder, an unmatched overcoat, and the mid-seventies' physical frame alighted from the train and walked slowly toward the exit. The town's Railway Station, recently painted with a pleasant color patch, adages and slogans decorated the walls and some quotes from the town's grandfathers spreading their thoughts and dreams of the town. His eyes riveted for a very long time on these catchy creations.

The town was geographically a small port with its old lighthouse beaming dim light across the sky, with trawlers and old rowing boats at anchor, the economy restricted to its livelihood of fishing, ferrying merchants with their stock-in-trade and travelers, and little movement of forest timber and agricultural produce. Though not very dense, tall trees with thick foliage and offshoots of different greeneries, the historical monuments explained proudly of its heroes in building its culture and heritage while protecting the town from the cruel pillage of pirates and seafarers, and above all, the people's open arms reception to its guests. Oh, the gods would love to transcend from their heavenly abode to stay here for some time!

"Good, this station at last was made up," he noted gladly in his survey. There was yet a tinge of disappointment glancing from his expectation of why the gateway of his native town neglected until now was not made up long before.

"Sir, ticket please," a deep, rough voice rose from behind. Pulling his leather wallet from his old trouser pocket, the man said, "Here, young man," as he produced his journey reservation to the ticket examiner, who loudly read his name as "Brian, Nickolas 75" and quizzed the old man, who nodded his head in assent. The ticket examiner quipped, "Sir, with age we are growing while this town is now becoming young and fresh," and welcomed the inbound traveler courteously to the town as he returned the ticket to him.

Mr Brian, his young face mismatching his age and gait, and his slack dress resembling the sprites in Shakespeare's *Tempest*, came through the exit gate, surveying the portico where old and a few new cars were parked. He then looked around for his chauffeur, Christopher, who, leaning on a crooked and stunted tree and taking a puff from his cigarette, spotted this old man and assumed that Brian was his client for his cab.

Christy, short for Christopher, upstaged Brian's attention from the parking bay and queried,

"Mr Brian?" Christy nodded happily at his correct guess! "I am Christopher and I have come to take you to the cottage. Our car is parked in the bay outside a few meters from here. I hope you will not mind a little walk to reach our car." Brian took note of Christy's direct approach.

With one large carry bag stuffed in a second-hand car, Christy chauffeured through the town's lonely streets, the tall trees on both sides blocking the sky, a small river with her feminine and elegant curvaceous grace streaming along the motorway. The colorful parrots, white and gray doves, and tiny sparrows chirping all over the atmosphere, puppies, rabbits, bulls, and donkeys scurrying, with a stray peacock spreading its iridescent feathers dancing in tune to the pleasant atmosphere all through the outskirts, guided the chauffeur in his driveway, sometimes crisscrossing or taking a direct flight en route to Brian's cottage. Following these natural guides, Brian enjoyed the birds' pleasant company and cool breeze.

Brian disembarked with his carry bag at the cottage and immediately settled in the lounge. "That was a long driveway," he said to himself.

Refreshing himself from the tiresome journey with a lukewarm shower and a light morning breakfast, along with a large mug of black coffee, Brian reclined on the porch just a little outside his cottage, enjoying the serenity of the surroundings. The dogs with their puppies, cats, and kittens, and sheep and lambs wagging their small tails on the dew on the top layer of the fresh grass offshoots along the pavements created a buzzing morning. The straying cows and bulls, cars and people moving lazily contrasted a false picture of abundant time at their disposal.

Engrossed in this melee, Brian slowly resumed his pastime - slumber - specifically, morning sleep! A few ticks and the gong of the town's huge clock jerked him awake to get ready for the day.

Brian was walking along the market and paused at the Four Road Junction, so named because the arterial roads from each direction converged at this point. He looked around to decide which way he wanted to go next.

There, he was happy to see his Alma Mater, The Premier Montessori & Higher Education School, and the building, too, that aged just like him. The students coming out of this institution, like bright sunlight, spread to take roots at all corners of the globe and reach the peak of their careers, stamping their identities in the social register.

Brian was a little sad to take particular note that nobody took a personal interest in visiting his Alma Mater. Probably his predecessors might have contributed their mite during their visits, of which he might not have been aware. He consoled himself and took a detour as he longed to see his classrooms.

The meager contributions from local ex-students, government bodies and donations from social institutions barely kept its survival to continue and churn out fresh minds into sterling and high-quality students every year.

Brian decided to meet the School's Managing Council the next morning.

As he walked through the market, which, with the passage of the town's administrative plans and implementations, still remained in its infantile development, he noticed an old nameplate 'N R R Cloth Stores', hanging precariously at the entrance of the old building. He remembered that it was here, after schooling, that he started his part-time job in his teenage years. The local laws then did not permit underage employment.

Probably, it might have been the universal call for violation of local laws for employment of tender-age or adolescent students in the marketplace! What is not clear is whether any social sanction or legal approval was ever tacitly accorded universally for such underage labor. If not, how did underage employment flourish even in civilized societies under vigilant legal eyes?

Vividly remembering, Brian after Physical Training and National Cadet Corps classes every evening up to 4.30 p.m., rushed home to change his school uniform and with crumpled casuals put on, worked as a helper up to 9.30 pm, stretching sometimes up to 10 p.m. all seven days in the shop in the early '70s for a paltry twenty-five cents a day that would allow him to buy eggs and bread at the end of the day. He was the only underage boy able to read, write, and speak the local lingo while the other tall, macho, and regular employees were all sort of ruffian salesmen.

With these earnings at the end of his work and on his return way home, he usually bought some flat breads, ketchup, and other household food and groceries for the next day. Oh, that was indeed a hectic life, yet he was content with it and simply enjoyed it!

With the sunset and night slowly creeping in, Brian returned to his cottage and after dinner to his heart's content, he unconsciously slumped into sleep.

The next morning dawned with a fresh breeze and birds' lively chirping sounds. Brian, unaware of how long he had slept, opened his drowsy eyes slowly to check the clock, which was then chiming at nine.

He had hurriedly done his brushing and bathing all at once, finished his breakfast of some old bread loaves filled with a piece of bacon, some green salad and layered with flavorsome small sugar candies, had a large mug of black coffee, and set out to his Alma Mater.

With his long and fast-paced steps and his mind now eager like a baby to reach its mother but still anguished at not reaching her at that moment itself, Brian gazed up at the sky and looked either ahead or sideways without any purpose.

Seeing the school children parading, walking in groups and solo along the way, he felt, "Ah, I know what my life means now!"

The small children slowly walked, middle and higher-grade students and their class teachers hurriedly pouring in, the school echoed its reverberations all over the town at half-past nine. Standing outside the gate of the school building, he looked at some school children hopping and running to reach school before the first ring of the school bell and the closure of the school gate. It was a very pleasant sight, too, and a good treasure to experience again the lively green memory of his school days. More than the fresh memory, Brian transported himself along with those children competing in their running.

Reliving his glorious school days, Brian's nostalgia returned to his favorite classes and teachers.

Mrs Wilma Gomes, who took the English and Maths classes, was his all-time favorite tutor and a guide right up to the completion of his schooling. "We often misuse adjectives and adverbs more than the use of correct words," Mrs Gomes had been pounding on him, especially at the same time other students who needed a little brushing in her class. He remembered with tears rolling down his cheeks her strenuous efforts on correct pronunciation, delivery of proper dialects, and effective writing of English as a medium of language for communication of thoughts and ideas in their entirety. Her English tutorials were always a pleasant learning for all the years, more for himself and even today, than for all of his other brilliant classmates.

"Oh my God, that was Mrs Gomes again, coming to teach maths." In Maths, she taught basic formulas, theorems, and rules, guiding them all the way up to more complex problem sums.

Mrs Gomes, one of the most senior and experienced faculty members, enjoyed her profession. She was often deputed to conduct the classes of other faculty members during their vacation. Through her method and approach, she became the students' favorite teacher, and the students sought her out even after her retirement in their quest for knowledge!

Mrs Gomes was very objective in that those maths students who were able to complete the class assignment could leave after the class period was over; however, the students who were behind in their class assignment were compulsorily instructed to stay, complete the task, and then attend their other classes. No, there was no court of appeal!

This kind of impasse brought the brilliant students to help the less talented students understand the maths problem and then work together to arrive at the correct answer so they were able to attend the other classes. A novel way of bringing all students together, and Mrs Gomes scored a double win!

Then, there was the 'commandant' Vensan Eyar, nicknamed by students for imposing his militaristic discipline, teaching all three science subjects: Biology, Chemistry and Physics. He showed species of plants and animals in his biology class and demonstrated the properties and functions of physics and chemistry with appropriate lab experiments.

In the early days, the special and additional extra coaching was only at the house of the class teacher, totally given free to needy students – there was no barrier and any student could easily meet the class teacher after school hours – with just one condition to do all the remaining homework in his presence.

At the repetition of a mistake, the class teacher tightly clenched his fist and pounded endearingly on the head of the student. Though this scene looked awfully dreadful, the result was amazingly rewarding. There was an overall positive turnabout in that even all the 'so classified' dull students seated in the last benches too developed a liking for learning, and that was the most important encouragement for tutors for all their efforts to school the children.

This culture of a personal bond between Alma Mater and pupils had quite an enriching resonance, much contrary to current professional coaching institutes, perhaps the highest form of craziness to separate students from faculty. Sadly, neither gained anything from the personal bond nor from learning!

Abruptly, he realized the important purpose of his school visit.

He dashed into the chambers of the school's current principal, Mr Wasan, and through the cabin attendant sent a message on a small slip of paper to him for an immediate meeting. Brian, after waiting for a short while, was called in and asked to be seated opposite the principal. The nameplate read E. N. Wasan, M.Sc., M.Phil.

"These days, a high academic qualification is a prerequisite at every level," he wryly smiled.

The Principal, coming from the adjoining cabin, entered his chambers through the back entrance. He appeared in his early forties, tall and slim, with bifocals loosely resting on his bulging brown nose. His personality resembled that of an ex-warfare veteran and he conducted himself straight to practicality.

Brian introduced himself as a student of this prestigious institution three to four decades ago. Brian continued, "Sir, I am still proud that I studied here and spent my school days in this institution. My association with various faculty members was, by and large, learning at its real meaning."

"We, of course, underwent corrective measures and punishments that were meted out to us. We never knew until now that such punishments were essential to strictly streamline our focus in our learning aptitude within the academic term."

"Yes, we ignorantly rebelled and revolted and with their forbearance, the teachers wanted us and indeed helped us establish our identity with our heads held high in the current world of disorder enmeshed with greed and lethargy overflowing. This school goaded us to stand out against the bleak prospects of sustenance and human security from every front and to come out unscathed."

"I, for all my classmates, acknowledge gratefully, but that would not compensate adequately in any way. Our desire for education ignited manifold only from this institution even after our exit," Brian's face showed all of his pure emotions, and his eyes glistened.

"I have come here to help restore the regal face of my Alma Mater and repair it to its original decor. I want to meet the executive member of the managing council who would be able to take appropriate and expeditious action. Could you please direct me to him?" Brian concluded his purpose of the visit.

Moved by the intensity of Mr Brian, Wasan rose to bow his head and extended his hand in a warm gesture, saying, "Sir, this school is very fortunate with your visit after so many years, and it is a lot of happiness for us to have you as one of its alumni members."

"I am the executive member of the Governing Board of this school," he continued, "I have the power to act and do all that is fair and necessary as far as the administration and academic curricula of this school are concerned."

Brian, while handing a token check of twenty-five grand dollars along with his contact details to the Principal, Mr Wasan, said, "Sir, it is my privilege and I will be visiting you periodically and essentially to see my Alma Mater. Please see that the old profile of the building is restored to its majesty."

He then took some liberty and went around his classes on the first, second, and third floors. He was unable to contain his raw childhood jubilation, which was now overflowing, and at the same time, he was inexplicably hesitant to leave the premises.

Just out of the school premises, "Now what?" Brian asked himself and wanted to glance at his school playgrounds. His legs carried him aimlessly through the eastern sector along the beachfront, half a furlong just away from the school.

He saw a few fishing boats mooring in, the fisherfolks' high-pitched banter, trawlers, and motorboats speeding ahead of one another, and the lighthouse at the mid-sea beaming its rays farthest in the day too. He stood there wishing to cling still on to his childhood.

Seeing some of the stout passers-by, Brian suddenly remembered his Physical Training Instructor, Mathew. He was frolicsome but a taskmaster and was nicknamed Macho Mathew. In his period of PT drills and exercises, all class students assembled at the school's largest playground stretching its length and breadth over one mile outside the town and through the bamboo, coconut, and tall palm trees extending their pinnate leaves, crabs running and conch and shells scattered.

Across the ground ran the narrow rail tracks and a freight train passed by. Sometimes in the twilight, our village folks and young children sat on the rail tracks, gleefully gossiping and discussing their topics while munching peanuts, popcorn, and other treats. At other times, they shooed away the cattle and other animals from their reserved seats, a delight to live by!

The PT instructor was tall and stout, his right hand swinging a wand back and forth. He was a sight of fear that would invite the students' involuntary participation in sports and drills. 'No more' was a word only in their academic vocabulary, but the students stayed energetic with their toned-up physique until the completion of their schooling.

In some inclement evenings when the sun was still warm, he took the students to the beach and drilled them to run barefoot for a full half an hour along the wet but warm sands, and that was how the boys learned to sprint. Probably Ben Johnson did not meet this taskmaster; else the sprinter would have definitely broken more of his own records!

Besides the daily drill, the PT instructor, accompanied by other teachers, took the school students to various local picnic spots, museums, bird sanctuaries, and other heritage places, explaining the importance of each place. He had a special talent for bringing both boys and girls together. He cajoled and exhorted his students - both boys and girls - to extensively train in the chosen vocal and instrumental music competitions.

Imagination, human care, and clear vision are all embedded in his upright personality, 'Macho Mathew'!

The sun was setting in the blue waters, and the sea wind was breezing with sands across. Brian stretched himself with both hands laid under his head. "I will definitely not get another opportunity to enjoy this affable Mother Nature," he said aloud, with his eyes closed to prevent the breezing wind from spraying sand granules.

He was hovering over some of the past grizzly nightmares as if he was seeing his old uncle and aunt pushing him to do something that he did not want to do, sometimes a stray unicorn appeared from nowhere, sounding a high-pitched neigh, thick white goats bleating and a pack of jackals and wolves ready to pounce on him, angels urging him to continue his journey, and the dreary ghosts taking him through dark and dense space.

He sweated profusely in the backdrop of the cool sea breeze, unable to read the clear meaning of all these dreary nightmares. He tried to recapitulate various events, friends, and all other known acquaintances chronologically and made frantic attempts to connect to this nightmare, as far as possible. Sadly, he let these visuals go, yet they continued to ring in his mind!

This flash overshadowed his jubilation, and he trod slowly to his inn. Returning to his inn and much against his longing for delicious variety, he had his stale dinner. All along, he was trying to find what his mind's forewarning was about, and unable to do so, he thought, 'Maybe later days will unfurl the answer or maybe this is his mind's hoax'. The day's hectic schedule slipped him into a deep sleep.

'Dr T S V Cherry, B.Sc., M.B.B.S., General Practitioner', the smudged whiteboard read outside an old building, housing his personal clinic. A malnourished boy stepping briskly in his gasp entered the clinic and he was accosted at the entrance. The doctor said, "You are, as usual, late today. There, the patients are waiting for a long. If you can, talk to them and try to find out something about their illness and send them one by one to me."

The doctor, with his outstanding professional skills and caliber, was too swift to read his rural patients and cure them of their seasonal illnesses, physical abnormalities, and psychological aberrations. Probably he drew inspiration from the current generation of Sigmund Freud of Austria and Carl Jung of Switzerland on their specialization in neurology, as well as on the myriad functioning of the mind. The Father of Surgery, Sushrut, around 800-700 B.C. in ancient times in India, was his constant model.

This underage lad was none other than our Brian, now working as a trainee in the clinic as the school's annual examination got over and vacation commenced.

Brian was given the additional assignment of coaching the youngest niece of the doctor. The girl, charming in her appearance, well dressed in her faded green shorts with a yellow T-shirt on top, was studying in the eighth grade, three grades lower. "Hi, you look pretty good. What is your name?" asked Brian, using all his unrefined charm. "Amanda," she replied coyly, perhaps she met a boy for the first time outside her school as well as her family. She looked brilliant, radiating an aura, and she just did not need coaching in her studies at all. Brian was amused as to why the doctor insisted on coaching this girl.

A few students had the privilege of a tour to pre-planned destinations and visits to their close relatives during their vacation, while the majority of students, without any choice, whiled away their time in the market, beach, common library, and parks.

Brian noted that some affluent children were forced to engage in extra activities against their will. Their affluent environment fostered a streak of inferiority complex in his mind, caused by his appearance, crumpled dress, and economic status. This was probably the first instance from which his inferiority complex firmly took root in his mind, manifesting strongly then and now. This helpless state of his living irked him to a great extent.

Brian remembered his last joyous vacation in the not-so-recent past. Brian and his three friends, while boarding the new dome bus at a local Oregon bus terminus on their pleasure trip, were so excited. Not because of their journey to see around, but essentially because they traveled in a new dome bus that provided elevated and panoramic views of the bus route, miniaturizing the buildings, carts, passers-by, and even the tall trees. Brian and his friends were hyperactive, looking up at the sky and around, and straining a little to look sideways and backward through the dome. Like small babies that tasted the first drop of honey, they yelled at one another, "Hey, look at that half bus there," pointing to a single-decker, and their joy contagiously percolated to other passengers as well.

Even old and affluent people had this peculiar fad and traveled in a new dome bus to get the outside views of scenic greenery and the jolly movements of passersby while reliving their childhood, their sense of culture abandoning them ruefully.

Alighting from the bus at the destination, Brian and his troupe looked around and reached a small open market to buy pastries, coke, and beer cans to satiate themselves a little.

Brian had a keen eye for observation on the passing scenery, birds chirping and gliding, regulated traffic blaring horns at the congestion, and long waits at the road signals and they all derived elated sense during their bus journey which they missed while walking as one among the pedestrians typically with a mobile in one hand and a half-munched pastry in the other.

The pedestrians walking ahead and some at the signal junction looking anxiously for the green light to cross to the other side of the road, some chitchatting, hollering and murmuring with one another and among groups, some differently crippled old people with static faces in their wheelchairs and crutches looking at the passers-by or around, suitcases on castor rollers and trolley carts, backpacks and sling bags winching along, this is a spectacular scene of a chaotic normal day, yet one of the joyous moments not to be missed at all.

The noon sun went berserk with all its penetratingly blazing rays, yet people accustomed to its tantrums were unmindful of its scorching temper. From nowhere, the black clouds surged stealthily along the southeast skies to drizzle down in an attempt to cool the hot climate. The people then realized and looked up to see from where those water droplets came.

That was his first and perhaps last luxury of his vacation!

Working as a trainee in the clinic, he was methodically ingrained in the properties of various pharma chemicals and their effects on the admixture of different compounds, patients' general illness, correctly reading the doctor's scribbled prescription, administering the right dosage of pills, capsules, and medicinal syrups, and, more importantly, collecting the medical fees as per the tariff. For Brian, though an underage schoolboy, the training was strenuous and equally fascinating!

At the end of the day's work, he would give a summary of which medicines were distributed, and stocked out for immediate replenishment, together with an account of cash collections, while handing the soiled and crumpled currencies to the doctor.

For such a tedious job of two and a half hours in the mornings and five hours in the evenings all seven days, Brian, as a trainee, got at the end of a month's labor, a paltry pay of fifteen dollars. When Brian vented his dissatisfaction, the doctor's stern reply was, "You are underage and a trainee now. You cannot be employed on a regular pay scale. With this wage, you try and finish up your education. Once you complete your education, come back and we will see how best and where we can fix you." The doctor dismissed him disdainfully.

It was at this time that Brian realized that unclassified exploitation was engaged in every legalized field, whether fancy shopping centers, medical institutions, or service centers. This couldn't be stalled or overcome unless he pursued to complete his studies.

Discussing this matter with some of his friends during the weekend, Brian was asked to take up technical educational training. Though this was, he felt, a good suggestion to suit his caliber, his precarious living did not offer that much privilege of affordability to follow.

Francis Rogers, one of his siblings whom he met quite occasionally, told, "Brian, you will get only peanuts for all your labor from such personal employers. Try and find out if you can and join a private company where you get decent pay even as a trainee for all your labor. Maybe you have a bright chance for a permanent role. Roger, your idea is bright, but who will take an underage boy like me?" Brian questioned.

"There is one way and I don't know, Brian, if ever it will work out fully to our expectation. My dad is a JAO, Junior Administrative Officer in the power distribution company, 'NES plc' and I will try during our dinner time and request him to help you his best in his capacity. Maybe you will get a breather, or maybe not at all." Roger was practical in his reply to him.

If you are a good observer, you will be quite fortunate enough to realize that young teens' friendship is pure, uncomplicated, and strong. Outside contamination has the least chance to seep and cause ripples with its venomous impact of social discrimination.

As we grow up influenced by unbalanced personal choices and desires, our first scapegoat at the sacrificial altar is our genuine teenage friendship, the easiest and cheapest bargain for greed and personal prejudice. This first sacrifice takes sweet revenge on our foolishness in our tottering old age, by churning out fresh memories of our teenage friendship day in and day out. And then, we continue to rue our current inability to correct our foolish decisions and restore that genuine friendship!

THREE 'P'S - (1) PERSPIRATION

Every underage lad goes through such a despondent situation, unable either to continue studies or land in, if not lucrative, commensurately paying job to sustain his growing years. Brian often resorted to borrowing from his elderly friends, obliging their personal and household errands. It was not a pay-out but a loan to be repaid, often on unjustifiable personal demands. The cruel days sometimes urged him to take a real bowl for alms, but, thank Heavens, his big proud Self raised itself standing between the 'Now' and his 'future'.

Walking down a long stretch of muddy road, the sun gleefully scorching his skin along the way, withering a cluster of green and brown leaves and branches on the roadway, not another day would ever dawn to feel Mother Nature's cool and gentle hug. The black clouds, not blocking the sun altogether, but partially covering it, gave some respite from the sweltering heat.

For Brian, the coming few days passed drastically slowly and what was then eons or ages meant had now become clear to him!

"My early childhood days are frighteningly anguishing. Oh God, bless the other children of my age with, if not wholly, at least a little comfort in their childhood to contend with their daily living," all his frustrations pleaded loudly.

Eagles circling high above and crows competing in the sky, dogs barking and looking in alacrity, running helter-skelter to escape from the municipal veterinary vans, and agile cats regally crossing the lanes while mulling over why their tiger cousins still pry yonder in the forests, with so much noise and so many activities buzzing around, Brian haggardly counted his steps forward.

Ruminating on where to go, how to hunt for a job, or whom to see for some help for his livelihood, how long and how far he would be able to stretch himself with this nomadic wandering were some of his mind rumblings. Brian had no answers and eked out his life!

His contemporaries, some herding thin and frail cattle, a few others engaged in tilling parched soil, weeding, and irrigating all side by side to complete their work before the sunset, and a few more drawing water manually from wells for their homes, depict a vivid farm life. Sitting atop the trees, the schoolboys played like monkeys, jumping and running around, while girls happily sat under the tree shelter licking the raw mango and plum tamarind seeds that the boys plucked from the trees. Oh, what a chirpy atmosphere under the shade of the trees with passing winds!

Fatigue and famish enveloped him, and with the scorching heat continuing its onslaught, he felt, "This has got to end now." A streak of a smile like a crescent splashed across his face, and he heaved a sigh of comfort as the sun cascaded down the sky, with cool twilight surpassing.

He looked around as he continued until he reached the crowded town market. The darkness seized the alley. Brian glanced at a few street corner shops, vendors, large warehouses that traded in retail wares, and roadside eateries which were famous in the Far East nations and were sprouting in the Western culture too and eyed a bleak chance for some labor or contract work offered here or elsewhere.

A surge of impulse he felt and he suddenly barged into "Johnson's Book Stall." It was a medium-sized mansion, depicting the yore Pantheon structure with hand-carved Greek doors. Johnson's Book Store was distributing medium-sized children's storybooks, toys, games, and some magazines and newspapers for local customers. The bookstall owner, a Greek, slender and fair lady, Miss Ariane, spotted the pathetic Brian opening the door to step in. "Hey you, stay there! What do you want here in this bookstore?" the lioness roared, and Brian was taken aback.

The long walk and anguish for a job or some help drained his stamina to speak clearly, yet he mumbled, "Madam, I am Brian, looking for some job to stay alive." Ariane felt moved by empathy for him and thought for a moment what to do with Brian. She took a swift decision, rather an uncalculated risk, and offered him a job as a retainer to do errands in the store, on low wages. She instilled a few morals in him, like honesty and life goals to chase within a specific tenure. "So, that will give you meaning for your life!"

Brian was surprised by her genuine intent to help and guidance. Yes, God is there!

He had, at the same time, noticed a little solace inexplicably transcending over him to relieve his distress of long-suffering.

"Ah, Brian is now steady and will be happy to get his daily meal," is what his well-wishers felt, and they breathed a sigh of contentment. Brian, to sustain his new assignment, put in more effort on his part to know about his job – like what type of books were stacked and where, how to sell what he has got against his customers' choice, and where to source to satisfy customers' demands. In addition, he took it upon himself to run between book publishers and distributors, power and statutory payments, and bank and office accounts. Besides, he was keen on upgrading himself with the decorum of customer relations.

Ms Ariane's words to set and follow his future goal for a purposeful and satisfying living were still ringing in his ears. Though he drew a blank on what she meant by her suggestion, he felt it wiser to seek her help later. His dedication extended beyond his stipulated working hours to take stock of what was done and what he would need to do to meet his growing job demands.

He slept barely a few hours and was always at the call of his job. The exacting stress would have knocked the natural senses of other vagrant and fragile youth of the same age level, but Brian quite effortlessly moved through it.

His singular aim boosted the sales of the bookstore and its growth. With each passing day, the number of patrons increased, and he successfully befriended some loyal customers in his profession. This necessitated him to seek other open and optional venues to nurture the bookstore. The next few months saw a gradual expansion of the bookstore operations in school stationery, writing instruments, and sports utilities. The bookstore peaked its sales performance, and Brian too happily advanced his comforts.

That opened some quite electric moments to stay with his friends in his spare hours also. Meeting each moment and discussing with his friends on books they read and their other activities was the routine of his extended life.

Days fast slipped and good friends turned into a source of bad influence. They plotted evil designs and encouraged him to indulge in poker games, movies, and other frittering ways. In the beginning, it was a novel experience for him. Without ever trying to check the motives of his friends, Brian became subservient to their whims, and he was misguided to neglect his whole livelihood.

The queer turns of life sponged his brisk work-life balance which he devotedly built until now. As one unknown genius once said, *"Humans are slaves of physical comforts,"* Brian, too, enjoyed his present moments extensively, and he subscribed generously to the veracity of this adage. With that, he developed an evil tendency of whiling away his productive time with his friends and, like a sot, neglecting all his precious self.

Every good beginning has to have its unavoidable ending. Brian, abandoning his regular work and neglecting his discipline, brought upon himself to be out of his employment. He ended up a vagabond, wasn't that the irony of fate? He returned to his earlier despondent days!

Gauging his friends for their propensity to support him in his downtrodden days, he learned about the tricky human selfish nature. He sulked and lamented over his own doings and vowed to steer clear of all his dispensable appendages. He charted a plan to identify all those that were to be weeded out and, in their place, to adopt positive habits and a dependable coterie of advisers and colleagues.

(2) PERSISTENCE

He consulted his new friends and looked up creative ideas that would provide him with a source for his livelihood. Some friends obscurely suggested enrolling in the army, police, or public transport service and elaborated numerous ways to a 'no-destination'.

"To err is human." We humans need an umbrella for our lazy attitude! Whether we make up next time or not, we still exist quiescently. Conversely, Brian rose again from his slumber and learned a rich lesson from his recent mistakes!

With elderly people's nondescript suggestions and ideas pouring in, Brian took to launch his own business venture in the retail trade of building materials and made friends with building and construction people in the locality. For an initial period of three to four months, the business flowed smoothly, and Brian was quite happy about his new profession. With the market economy sliding, crunching credit terms from his suppliers and defaulting payments from his buyers wrought many tormenting and sleepless nights for a novice in the trade to meet supply and demand. He shut his shop ultimately with his books of accounts in the red.

Francis, his cousin, came again to the rescue. Based on his avid interest in social services, Francis told him to 'just start' taking old people across the road, drop the school-going children, provide some medical help, and expand your services gradually. 'You will then get to know your life's path'.

Above every other adult passer-by, the children had an extraordinary remembrance and affectionate reception for their friend, Brian. Besides these children, aged and quavery people waited a little longer until Brian arrived at the spot to escort them to their destination, an unclassified bond and expectation gradually increasing between them.

Involving himself with society's anchor of children and senior citizens brought him to build acquaintances with rich, influential, and powerful people entrenched in public services, education, local maintenance, and administration. Brian provided, in servility, his help to perform their social commitments.

While climbing his way slowly up, he took, as a first step, a small batch of adolescent students and meticulously trained them to form efficient traffic marshals chiefly to ensure the safety of children, seniors, and aged pedestrians at the zebra crossings, besides regulating traffic movement. Within the next few months, he regained their confidence and respect to bag the society's "Peace de Corp" to promote effectively, maintain, and improve the society's various economic, administrative, and cultural facets.

This social welfare activity recognized the town's tacit approval of his efforts. The other elite pillars of the society, from the medico fraternity, architecture, and construction stalwarts to legal and financial wizards, who earlier relegated him as though he were a pariah, now wholeheartedly befriended him to use his services in their important cultural and economic functions. Of course, that was one of their promotional ways to boost their fiefdom; this was an uncharted foray till now.

Brian was growing to shoulder and to finely tune the town's whole serenity in the backdrop of his acumen and his attitude to rise like a phoenix. With his sheer stint of complete involvement, he formed a team of dependable and talented workforce. He was arduous to chisel a name more particularly to erase his past and pave a platform as a prompt service provider in every house and a friend much sought after.

Mr Howard Ruth, short and bulky in his mid-thirties, bespectacled, with a half-burned cigar puffing out grayish smoke like George Stephenson's first steam engine, his masculine hands stretched across the armrests, was reclining wholly on the cozy chair. One of the town's politico bigwigs, Ruth was, at his very young age, entwined in spheres of roads, construction, and a set of other high-potential activities.

In his childhood, he was a big ruffian, squeezing his classmates on his chosen errands of fetching cigars, golfer's tees, hockey clubs, balls, and drinks from the school mess, ostensibly playing his whimsical tunes. His classmates were in awe of his affluent living; if anything, his academic proficiency and his caliber were always like a notebook's brand new pages!

He was culturally a prominent figure, depicting and establishing his all-powerful stature in all social media. He had manufacturing interests in medical formulations, health and hospital services, construction of buildings and roads, warehouse and transport insurance, and an unsecured big money lending business. His henchmen were involved in illegal sand mining, adulteration of food products, spurious drug making, and seizing properties for defaulted loan repayments.

Ruth projected himself successfully as a philanthropist and a guardian of downtrodden people in society. The naive poor people were cheated by his alluring pretensions and were losing irretrievably their means of support like their pieces of farming land, oil tilling facilities, grazing cattle and sheep, houses, fish boats and trawlers, woven clothes, bed sheets, and carpets from the looms, and other supporting occupations of their existence. He was immensely enjoying slavish patronage unsolicited from various strata of educated, influential, and social pillars.

Ruth looked intently into the eyes of Brian like a tiger aiming at its prey. Brian, feeling a chill surging through his spine, failed to return Ruth's gaze daringly and looked elsewhere. In the end, Brian submissively listened and never attempted to even glance at Ruth throughout the meeting. Brian has to acknowledge this flaw!

Ruth was very warm and said, "Mr Brian, our townsfolk appreciate your teamwork here. It is a good sign that a young and enterprising lad like you takes an interest in our town's developmental work. Quite a vast number of youth have enrolled under your supervision to do that social work, and that is definitely your noble intention and talent, right?"

"We have three huge ongoing projects. These projects include dilapidated buildings, a crematorium, adjoining burial grounds on the outskirts of the town, arterial passages to our town on all sides, and other repair and development work, with the most prestigious being the hospital building."

"This, we feel, is not up to the whole of your fresh talent as this entails a vast labor force, compliance with local law, enormous capital and would make you a spend-force to be deported to the backyard of the Society. To begin with, you should start your activities from the outskirts of the town. Probably this is what you need now and as you grow with experience, you will get a clear map of direction. You will then qualify for all big projects."

Pensively, he thought for a moment and surmised that his independent work style was being bridled. Just after a few soporific seconds, he regained his composure and spoke, "Sir, all the jobs you have listed to me now belong to building and construction specialists. I strongly believe that they have full insight into the pending status of these jobs and their acquaintance with contract laborers. They might enhance your prestige and popularity in society with their craftsmanship."

"So, Sir," Brian summed up, "it is my humble recommendation to you that such experienced people be assigned to this whole job. Their expertise will save a lot of time and money, and we will get solid and grand structures all around our town." That was quite good reasoning, so Ruth admittedly nodded his head!

Ruth, while dismissing Brian's logic, proposed, "Mr Brian, we know that well. Some professional stalwarts will join your team to accomplish this work by the end of October to comply with stipulated schedules, and you will take adequate care of our interests." Oh, what a brute!

Brian felt the burden of a big boulder on his shoulders. His mind all of a sudden became numb. Brian, in a mix of feelings and frustration, just exited Ruth's chamber.

"What the hell is happening around me here, and why can't I do my work in my own way?" he let out a scream, unable to tame his mind's loud wailing. His protuberant eyes were bloodshot.

In an attempt to regain his sobriety, he decided to go for a stroll, much against his mind. Sighting the sun ascending to its peak and the sultry climate exhaling hot air, he was at a discomfort, unable to control his temper to curse the natural elements. He stroked his hair tenderly to start his usual and open dialogue with his mother, Nature. A few dull seconds swiftly passed by and looking at the blue horizon, he was experiencing a peculiar serenity he just could not fathom, which was soothing his troubled mind. A wave of cool and gentle breeze caressing his face with its musical humming soothed his violent mood swings and helped him strut in his characteristic persona.

Is he a born fighter or a selfish coward buckling under pressure? Time alone will tell.

Brian, now fresh from his forty winks, wanted a cup of hot black coffee. Spotting a roadside vendor, he had his first sip and felt a bout of strength surging and fresh spirits soaring up in his body. Through vague memory, he remembered Ruth's irritating talk, his furious conduct at the meeting, and abrupt dismissal, and finally, the undesired work assignments given to him. He clearly grasped the situation that he was pushed to work under the supervision of the boss' abettor army.

Not knowing what actually needed to be done, Brian let go of him with a passing flow. Somehow, a ray of hope amidst the helpless chaotic situation glimpsed in his mind.

That, in the beginning, Brian would work alongside Ruth's professional team headed by Mr Quinton, a renowned contractor with job knowledge in hospitals, playgrounds, and schools, cultural centers, and core experience in cement mixing, concrete materials, and aptly employing labor to execute the job in grandeur style. Mr Quinton was assisted by two qualified construction and quality inspectors and a horde of contract labor teams for different work situations. Despite all fillings-in for the construction jobs as building activities gained momentum, the lacunae in basic structural design and foundation layout were quite obviously left out of the administrative approval. The chieftain did not notice at all.

While Ruth was happy to get his expert teams and Brian to work together, their casual approach to the job at hand was irritating to Ruth.

He summoned Quinton, his team with Brian, and spoke, "I am unhappy with you and your people's tardy and sloppy performance, Mr Quinton. The slow progress is another cause of our worry. This is your failure to bridge a cohesive rapport."

"We have entrusted this big job with due consideration of your talent and work experience. Alas, we are disappointed. You all are a part of our town! Our town's buildings, constructing a big hospital with advanced technologies and facilities, roads, and other projects are your responsibilities. You have to keep in mind that these prestigious public welfare schemes are a great boon to our town."

"I expect you all to put in more of your energy and time and work together to the best of your abilities to stick to the deadline. Please remember, you are not in your private construction business to work in the style as you wish." Dismissing his meeting with them, he warned seriously that "you will be held collectively responsible for your bad workmanship" to stick to the required quality and time deadline. "You fail and you will invite troubles," it was the undertone of a mafia thug!

Taking a cue from this disadvantage, Brian decided to act and convene a meeting with all workers. "Friends, we have now split the whole job into three basic departments."

"The design department will inspect the current state of the buildings, summarize the work to be done, and supervise the basic drafting, and final blueprint, in addition to being responsible for getting the required administrative approvals."

"The warehouse and storage department will take stock, ensure availability, and unhindered supplies of quality materials at the construction site."

"The masonry department is responsible for the actual construction work as per the schedule."

Brian reiterated Ruth's final warning vividly in his personal tone: "Dear friends, you all saw how our superior boss was disturbed, and, of course, you saw his controlled temper too. Lucky you all, the boss just left at that."

"I do not want to say anything more than what the boss expected us to do other than that you can exercise your freedom to work with us or walk out. Somebody may fill in your place and do much better and how difficult it is to live unemployed in this present scarcity."

"On account of such delays, all cost overruns on the company would be collectively borne by us. In turn, there would not be any wage increase or revision, God permitting, we stay with our spirits and health until completion of the projects."

Each department will work as a team and stay united. "So, dear team members, join us wholeheartedly. Do your work as per our guidance to finish the job, and I will see you continue here. Come, share your important personal problems with us, and we will try to find a solution for you." Brian, in his friendly way, assured his team over his boss Ruth's ire.

It was a clear sense of psychological burden on the whole team of workers. They assembled to hear Ruth in the first instance, hoping for a little hot beverage with some snacks.

All this while, Mr Quinton was speechless and a passive spectator while appreciating Brian's pep talk.

Then, like an arrow from a bow, Brian and Quinton sped to meet Ruth. "Mr Ruth, we spoke to our labor team and helped them realize the importance of our current projects and their delivery by the deadline. Due to Nature's fury, our townspeople have no proper shelter."

"Above all, it involves your prestige in society. So, I intend to take all your projects and the personnel under my care and supervision."

"I will guide them to complete the work orders under exacting demands. You may consider my proposal as you deem fit," so saying Mr Brian looked at Ruth. Wow, this was a new Brian with a fireball devouring the earlier indecisive and timid 'Brian'!

"Brian, if it is something like a common residential building or small repair work, I would gladly have given the job to you," Ruth replied matter-of-factly. "The professional experts find themselves unable to cope with their time and job demands. The local administrative council sticks to completion schedules, and every day their demands for job updates are increasing."

"Our present team under Quinton has years of vast experience to their credit and a good reputation in society. When they have failed until now, what can a novice like you do on such a prestigious project? That is our wild guess. Let us not waste any more time on futile exercises," Ruth said as he dismissed Brian.

Brian, a person not to be cowed down by such negative dismissals, trod along the line of Ruth, "You are right, Sir, their vast experience and good standing are the main causes of their failures. I have comparatively nothing to boast about."

"It is wise and the time is ripe to experiment with something new. So, I stake my prestige to complete this task," Brian again proposed rather submissively.

Thinking over his sustained persuasion and the importance of the proposal in the background of the loss of time until now, Mr Ruth rather selfishly considered that his prestige in the society was also at stake and was pushed to uphold it at any cost.

It also provided a clear chance for Ruth to project Brian as a sacrificial goat in the event of failure. Thus, Ruth acceded to Brian's suggestion and gave charge of the entire task with a clear and stern warning, "Brian, you fail, and you will run for your life from this town." Ruth just added a little more life to the adage, *"The man acts only when he is faced with no option."*

That was a small success, thought Brian as he collected all information on the pending status of work, labor, and stock registers, together with the available funds for the entire project, for his review. He then charted his work plan with some unforeseen exigencies.

He immediately convened a meeting and noticed that many faces were clouded with confusion and uncertainty. "We are well within our control, dear friends," began Brian to address the team. "The situation is not that bad at all. We will firstly get down to work and from there gradually go up with our daily work programs," his injection of adrenaline revived their sagging enthusiasm and their faces glowing cheerfully. He let the team members chalk out their weekly program to keep the timeline needed to be doggedly kept up, how many men additionally to be deployed, and their report was tabled before him to check and correct the faulty planning and identification of stage-wise specific areas of construction like the first plinth, entresol, stairways. All specialized labor was employed additionally to set the project concept to materialize into reality! He ensured that they all understood clearly and would collectively carry out the demands of their job. The momentum of the project now picked up, and Brian updated this status and subsequent work program to Ruth.

Sometimes Brian joined Mr Quinton and the entire or part of the labor force at their lunch table nonchalantly and created a jovial atmosphere to give succor to their strained mind and physique. This was one of his regular exercises, and he practiced precisely.

Oh, a storm was brewing in the deep sea! One of Mr Ruth's able assistants, Ms Cynthia, barged into the chambers of Brian and demanded to know, "Mr Brian, what is this I hear about you? How could you take over so abruptly from Mr Quinton? And why hasn't Mr Ruth considered me?"

Much against Cynthia's agitated mood, Brian was composed and relaxed to let the rough sea ebb a little and looked straight into her eyes. "Cynthia, the boss first thought of Mr Quinton on account of his vast experience. His failure to keep the ongoing status of the project upset the boss. The delay also caused capital block and time loss. To tide over the loose ends, I took my turn and then suggested to the boss about you. But then, thinking of the different construction requirements and close coordination with the labor force, the boss decided on me to experiment as a stop-gap arrangement."

"You are, of course, the natural choice for the job. Suppose you think you can do this job, shall I speak to the boss again? You may talk to him if you so desire at your discretion."

"If you alternatively think that it is appropriate for you to wait and take on a large project to suit your potential, why not then move along and cooperate with us in the current task? That way, this work experience will add some more credit to your eligibility in the coming days."

Somewhat pacified but not happy with the explanation given, Cynthia said, "Mr Brian, it's all right. You don't need to talk to the boss at this moment, and I will discuss with him when I get to meet him next time."

Collecting all rough sketches, Brian ran to the office of Ruth early the next morning and while placing them in the desired order of Mr Ruth, explained to him about the estimated cost overruns, work at different places, and the expected phase of completion by the end of each week.

"Sir, these are our draft plans. Please go through and examine as closely as you feel necessary. The final would be ready in a fortnight and with the stamp of your approval, that would be filed for the necessary approvals from the local government authorities. It would be helpful, Sir, to get the papers moved, with your influence, through the tables for their prompt approvals." From our side, we would be pursuing the matter with them regularly to satisfy their queries."

"Sir, The work would start thereafter. We would invite suppliers for negotiation and finalization of contract orders for the supply of labor, construction materials, transport fleet for men and materials, power supply back-up, and a recreation-cum-refreshment and lunch lounge for the workforce in accordance with existing stipulations and time schedules. We would call for an 'Earnest Deposit' of interest-free five hundred thousand dollars or a bank guarantee for an equivalent sum, with a clause for the forfeiture of 20 per cent of the order value as a penalty for short supply and short service.

"All updates will be posted to you at every stage; we will ensure proper controls," Brian summed up.

"The modifications or alterations in any of these projects at a later date would be difficult to implement, after the approval accorded by the concerned office." All such improvements need to be approved again by the local government. "We will still try to go with your suggestions on any such change you desire, and that can only be carried out as additional assignments with cost overlap."

Was Ruth dozing off or purported to be intently listening to Brian as Ruth fluttered her eyelids with an expressive sound 'tsk' 'tsk'? Brian, amazed to think, "Here, I am laboriously explaining my own projects and he is indifferent to me! Is that his way of working?" raising a shade of doubt! "Sir," Brian was direct in his question, "Are you not interested in these work details? If you have no interest in this project or if you do not wish us to proceed, please be open and clear in your message to us, and we will not bother you with our preliminary sketches."

"We would proceed only after your categorical clearance," so saying Brian returned to his cabin.

From the office of Ruth, Brian dashed to Quinton in his usual coffee tête-à-tête, explained the brief to Ruth, and his callous attitude to respond. He forewarned to stay until clearance to go with the project.

While keeping the day's episode at bay and trying to help Brian concentrate on other pending matters, Quinton discussed with him personnel deployment. "If Cynthia could be assigned to his department to facilitate the implementation of projects and in that process, she could enhance her creative talent. She would provide a much-needed fillip in the department," Quinton implored.

He called Cynthia to Quinton's office and said, "Well, Cynthia, these are the three prestigious projects we have on hand. The new hospital and its annex building, along with renovation work, repairing, and restoring dilapidated buildings in the central business avenue, and resurfacing roads from the outskirts up to our town entrance are current tasks. All these are important public welfare projects, and we have our reputation at stake in society."

"You may coordinate with Mr Quinton who will help you to pick your project to suit your passion and talent. You would at the same time be reporting to Quinton and extend all possible support to him. Please appreciate that Quinton is your immediate boss."

Brian, for a moment, felt as if he had hurt Cynthia and looked at her to say, "You would be responsible for your choice project and may coordinate with Quinton. Then, decide on your associates and colleagues to build your work team. Once you collect your workforce and draw your rough plans of stage-wise work, material procurement, and your other requirements, I need you to submit them through Quinton for my examination."

"Please be clear, we need to work within the available resources and mandatory structural requirements." Categorically spelling out what he expected from her, Brian looked at her rather questioningly.

Drawing inspiration from Brian, she weighed the options of projects available to her. Quinton discussed with her and helped her narrow her passion for construction activities, so she chose the repairing and restoring of dilapidated buildings. The idea of her choice was that, with the passage of time, the new project would add a feather or two to her credit for her career. Just to mold her capable of facing and tackling future challenges in designing and building different structures, Quinton involved her in the hospital project too.

She then took a site examination of all the twenty buildings of three-story condominiums and jotted down a list of work to refer to, review, and then repair to improve within the deadline. Cynthia then called her team to survey the existing status of the buildings.

She was disgusted to glance around stereotyped multi-storeyed buildings stacked like a pack of cards in a sartorial background. On conducting the exterior survey of old buildings, and in one encounter with a construction and building caretaker at the outskirts, Cynthia was afforded a chance to see the building layouts, material inputs, and other records. The documents clearly depicted the provision of facilities like a clubhouse, a swimming pool, indoor playgrounds, and parks and were endorsed with approval from the local authorities. These buildings lost their inhabitable worth not due to the passage of time, the visible cracks in outer walls, steel bars bent and slant, concrete masonry out of their installed locations, windows dangerously popping out, all contributing to an 'abandoned site' and slated for their demolition.

Taking a close interior examination, Cynthia noted blisters of the paint film, uneven ceilings and walls, poor sewerage outlets, and foul odor stemming from boxed-in kitchens and living rooms - in all, 'lack of maintenance' being the primary cause for such dilapidation. It was an eerie ghost town!

One more glance and the truth surfaced in the open. The promoters in their narrative promised a spacious carpet area, housing a large living room, kitchen, balcony, and restrooms over the livable area, an unfair bargain, future maintenance bills, and local mandatory payouts, at the cost of living space.

If some uncommon logic could prevail on the builders, a little more space would have been added to the matchbox tenements. That would infuse real human life moments which the new age family seldom spent together. This rare gift of 'family time' was cruelly appropriated.

A close look would reveal that all these self-acclaimed professionals, experts, and other tagged pros offered at your cost and against your uncompromising creative faculty just a little concrete space so that all living human beings became corpses while living there, without attachment and involvement to their tenements.

Cynthia took a close survey of what was sacrificed; it was not just the living space of the occupants for *the affluence* of builders and construction professionals. The cultural growth, wagging of sweet nothings, and sometimes spasmodic outbursts of neighbors forming 'pro and anti' groups, flavorsome delectable culinary exchanges between families hailing from different pastures and barren lands were stoned to cease. With all that, the howlers, creepers, quadrupeds, and jumpers tamed to lose their birth signature, the foliage in the background of tall skyscrapers withered to look like a sketch straight from the palette of a novice artist.Cynthia, on putting her survey report, suggested the demolition of all buildings in one go, which was easier instead of repairing and restoring all these 20 dilapidated structures. The construction of newer buildings would add greatly to the structural economy and its long tenure besides scenic beauty.

She supported her recommendation. "Probably, our forefathers from different religions and civilizations preferred living in thatched huts interlocked with tall coconut tree stems and leaves, bricks with bamboo and tree logs laid symmetrically, and soil-cemented houses in the mountainous terrains."

"The river's flow with small stones and pebbles, wood blocks, natural treasures, minerals, and resources along with breezing pure and cool air through all-weather assuaged our mental turbulence" solely for the good health of human beings.

At just a glance, Brian gleefully noted her intention and tenacity. "Cynthia, your plan looks good. Go ahead, include some margins to make up for unforeseen errors, and be critical of mandatory requirements and the time schedule," Brian decreed, like a Civil Judge in the court of law. It was a shot of adrenaline, and joy pervaded her!

In one of the daily round-ups of the buildings, Cynthia met Mr Shurman, a bald and bulky middle-aged man jogging zig-zag across the pavement. She was amused by his strides and initiated a conversation asking where he was residing and what his occupation was.

He was proud, without knowing who Cynthia was, to explain his locus standi in the area. When the redevelopment scheme was abruptly broached up for discussion, Shurman said that his wife was the secretary of the complex.

In the redevelopment of the large housing complex on a forty-acre plot with more than 300 affluent families, a devious Ulma Shurman, Secretary, and her confederate Huma Anderson, as president, on consistent liaison with Cynthia, brokered a scheme of redevelopment. With their sweet talks, cajoling, and intimidating, they sold their cunning plans and schemes convincingly both to the redevelopment corporate company and members of the complex. They were allured by ultra-modern facilities for less inhabitable areas against their eligibility, which was earlier recorded in the mandatory and approved local governmental layout of the building plans. The most senior Marketing Manager, Mr Richard, with vested operational power, collided with them at the sacrifice of his rationale.

The irony was that all accounts, administrative, legal, and other sundry works were being carried out at intervals convenient to him. A non-member and non-resident, imposing much of his clout and even in the society's meetings upheld his whims. The bona fide and non-participant members in the Managing Committee meetings bore his rude behavior. The local laws do not take cognizance of his willful tantrums, casting a blind eye!

As office bearers, Anderson and Shurman were responsible for all maintenance and cleanliness of the complex. Their motor cars were parked in their bay, and they went hopping and jumping over the garbage pile. Yet the clearing expenses of garbage soared month after month. Some members' voices calling for the clearance of such piled-up garbage went unheeded, with other members' attitude being "what about me?"

It was a pleasant Sunday morning. Shurman was feeling exuberant for no reason, gossiping and discussing with his friends animatedly on silly topics. They were enjoying themselves in a nearby cafeteria, with servings of their morning breakfast from a large tray neatly dressed with steamed dumplings, boiled vegetable salad, and a fresh green spinach leaf insert, along with a large mug of hot black coffee.

On his return from the cafeteria, he sensed sharp pins piercing along his left ribs, a little away from his left nipple. He was unable to locate the spot and determine the cause of the niggling pain. Upon reaching home, he frantically tried to speak to his medic but was given an appointment for the following day. His wife made a herbal concoction to relieve the pain, to no avail. It was a special Sunday morning overflowing with his natural spirits, but he now felt a dragging, dull moment with increasing pain, sometimes lessening to provide brief relief in a static posture. He diverted his mind to national news, sports, and other TV programs.

Funnily, all over the town, the 24 x 7 chemist outlets existed. In contrast, the emergency services, even on weekdays, were sparse and flung afar. The weekly Sunday holiday was always very important for the medico. For extreme emergency situations, the GPs and family physicians were unavailable at the first telephone call, and the excessive calls for emergency medical attention were a prime culprit resulting in negligence! The unlucky and suffering patients were forcefully pushed to reach the specialized hospital services.

In one of the well-equipped hospitals five kilometers away, there was an in-house medical attendant who was as crowded as any other normal working day with patients in the queue. By the time his turn came up for diagnosis, it was past ten at night, and he was admitted to the ICU for observation.

Calling Mr Quinton and his team immediately, Brian discussed the other pending hospital and road projects with clarity of purpose and direction and said, "Both the hospital and road repair work are very important public utility projects. We need to put in more concerted efforts. Our capacity is unlimited, and this is our best chance to show our model performance to stand with time." He then asked Quinton to submit his sketch of his working methodology for scrutiny and approval.

All this while, Brian's mind chanted 'performance and deadline', 'performance and deadline' repeatedly. For heaven's sake, he had to stay sane!

To inject and sustain working enthusiasm that in turn brings total commitment and to develop a joint work culture, he scripted the adage *"Forgive yesterday, tomorrow is all yours! Forget today, tomorrow forgets you!"* and attached one copy with various work plans and sent it to each superintendent. Such messages across all the work sites were displayed, and the townsfolk, who took delight in glancing at the signboard messages, were brimming with immense pleasure. "Ah, some work at last now slated to spring up," and in every nook and corner, the messages created awareness, and the local populace exuded a frenzied mood in the atmosphere.

Now what lies ahead is his big task of bringing all departments into full coordination with one another. These departments should be groomed to inculcate a sense of togetherness to work in tandem and to achieve economy with the best workmanship at the completion of the project.

Brian seriously dealt with delays, dereliction of duty, undue absenteeism, and all other negative causes that would very easily wrap up the tardy labor tendencies.

At the same time, he encouraged and disbursed awards and gift vouchers befitting their involvement and outstanding performance and brought to public recognition in the cultural and festival gatherings, especially to set a precedent to work and achieve the goal together.

Exceptional contributions were unfailingly marked for elevation up in the organizational ladder, in the form of a direct boost to one's capabilities and an outlet for the realization of personal growth, apart from an added financial package.

On regular inspection with Mr Quinton, Brian noticed some extra work put in by his team in the repair and development of roads and old buildings. "For the enormous experience and knowledge at your disposal," Brian addressed Quinton, "Sir, we feel your contribution in the past in the area of road repair and building resurfacing projects is highly commendable. Your concept and design deserve our appreciation." Cynthia too was present to mentally note this dialogue.

"Currently, both the old building and road projects come under increased daily usage with the general public, and these two projects need our priority attention and consolidated efforts for completion. The general public should not undergo any discomfiture," said Brian to his senior colleagues Quinton and Cynthia while approving the top-up provisions for additional men, material, and other utilities in proper line with their work estimates.

Brian returned the survey report on all old buildings with remarks and suggestions to Cynthia and the primary concept of building draft plans to Quinton. He spelled out clear directions that both would work cohesively and perform well above their job demands.

Cynthia carrying out her tasks efficiently as well, troubled Brian periodically on inadequate men and material problems, and he had diligently guided her to deal with problems hampering the construction of all old buildings, as though she were being shaped to assume after him. She already started entertaining dreams and aspirations. The human mind is indeed very kaleidoscopic in its aspirations!

When the plans and programs progress in toto as sketched, the human mind adapts to relax, enjoying serendipity. That, literate scholars and elderly experienced men too become victims, unable to attune themselves to *"discomfort is the basis of comfortable living"* is really cruel. The society's ivy league consisting of influential, wealthy business magnates and industrial leaders, leaving the general populace out and aside, is not at all an exception to life's anomalies!

Brian grew a 'persona gratissima' in the town. His increased social status against the backdrop of his uncompromising involvement fostered jealousy among his superiors and colleagues who were plagued by constant bouts of insecurity.

Greed and vices grew in equal proportion with elite society members, like weeds! Brian's work ethic and his stubborn attitude created an array of green-eyed monsters, devilish akin to Japan's recurrently lava-spewing volcanoes, among the top brass of the town's administrative cell, because of his continued denial of their selfish interests to fill their coffers from job contracts.

They waited breathlessly for an opportune moment to clip his wings and humiliate him so that he would not recover from his downfall.

They all together plotted different schemes and unscrupulous methods, in one way or another, to disgrace him in the eyes of society. Unscathed, Brian outsmarted them and their sinister schemes.

They just could not afford to 'dispense with him' forthwith because of his good relations with high-level acquaintances and staff in finance and administrative departments and his versatility. They cruelly set out to make him an essential puppet of their coterie to do their errands. Besides, they all feverishly desired to 'possess' him to prop up and consolidate their social image, as his service levels and involvement discerningly made him a magnetic charm of the crowd.

The ruling political power constantly engaged in stabilizing its game, neglecting the governance of law and order. This gave rise to instability gripping the society's finest texture of peace and growth. The wealthy and rich seized power to run the local climate whimsically, and this abrupt change worsened the living conditions, which until now were peacefully entrenched.

For the townsfolk, just a while ago, what was then a pleasant sunshine became a dark cloud and the expanse, not to be outdone by the social and political evil patrons, opening rhythmically with its lightning, thunder, and torrential downpour devastated the buildings, large road-crates, flooding arable lands, uprooting agricultural offshoots, the dead livestock scattered criss-cross with tree foliage, stems, and branches, the houses damaged and blown away all at one stroke. A wet foul odor closed the inhabitants' linear nostrils.

The next few days saw unclassified suffering - of all those distressed folks on the collapse of their intimate brethren siblings, piblings, niblings and friends, cats, dogs, and all living beings. Some boys and women were loudly yelling the names of their missing clan, with a furious attempt to locate their kids and kith - wailing on one side.

The town's administration swung into emergency measures to control the damage. The homeless people, crops, and animals were housed with the setting up of temporary shelters in schools, churches, and public convention halls. The social welfare institutions voluntarily moved in to assist in the town's uphill task and to provide succor with food, water, and clothes. The town's administration and the social institutions knitted together and with their economic reliefs for the sustenance of their people, though a huge task, provided a breather to all of the suffering people.

The economic structure shattered, rich and poor, literate and illiterate, known and unknown all merged into one common class - *orphan without care and identity.* Oh, what a divine justice!

Ruth with their cronies and Quinton catastrophically jolted and deprived of all affluence. They frantically ran from pillar to post for some financial support from the town's administrative wings for their survival. With available cash bills, all valuable stocks, finance, and estate documents stuffed in his Chrysler car, Ruth drove away to his safe haven, twenty-thirty miles away, accompanied by two of his security cronies.

Quinton, though he was an accomplice of Ruth, was not lucky enough to flee but was left in the lurch to defend himself.

Cynthia, unnerved by the cries, weeping, and cruel suffering of the people in the town and unable to cope with the chaos, moved surreptitiously to the other side of the town, seemingly with a practical mind!

The town's politicians en masse flocked to the other green pastures to save their skin from the deluge-ravaged town of 'Neigay', which was cut off from the mainland. The recent catastrophe brought the townsfolk to realize the need for a true leader who would steer them to the bright days of their life! Thus, the local people posted Brian as Interim President to oversee the administration of the town against his reluctance to shoulder administrative responsibilities which, for him, was a newer area.

In the midst of all this chaos, Brian managed to muster his sense and perseverance to stay put with his people and help alleviate their sufferings as far as possible. Just then a few of his loyal, young, and daring buddies joined him to restore the houses, wherein some repair work was already carried out making them habitable, to shelter the hapless victims. Step by step, they worked to pave and level the marshy alleys and roads for movement of the people and merchandise, with water and electricity supplies.

The continued high decibel of Brian's working buddies, on the other side to raise and disburse the relief among the suffering people, echoed through the clouds across the plains and mountains - what a stark contrast, noise in suffering and noise in hope!

Brian, seeing his efforts inadequate to provide the much-required level of relief, sent emissaries from his team to adjoining villages and towns seeking their help and cooperation and with ad hoc contributions in kind and cash to mitigate the sufferings of his townsfolk.

In rural villages, there was a custom based on the expectation to inquire with the postman and a courier delivery person if there ever was any mail, message, or parcel for a particular house or neighbor. The small children ran behind them for sheer joy.

Going through a similar childhood anxiety, Brian looked out if any person or help came forward for his town. He dejectedly hung his head low!

Until now, not much was expected of his efforts for help, and participation from the nearby towns and villages yielded hardly any fruit. The next morning's orange glow saw Brian and his townsfolk getting a fresh breather with a concurrent flow of support in kind and strong shoulders to rest their depressed emotions.

The sufferings of the people drove Brian to realize the urgent need for increased medical backup. He noted mentally taking up construction of the hospital building as his first priority.

Often we're conditioned to believe that our lives revolve around a great deal of what we do. But great moments catch us unaware and beautifully. Thanks to our neighboring towns for sharing and shouldering our plight!

"Now hath come the time," Brian engaged his entire team of buddies in the restoration and resurrection of the town's life. He split the entire team into four groups, each one assigned with buildings, hospitals, roads, and the last to fill in emergency calls. Working untiringly round-the-clock and attending the most important emergency calls for medical, police, water, and other departments, besides serving the local people, the entire team rose to create a gradual revival of faith, economy, and buzzing life to normalcy in the town. They deserved the angels' applause!

Cynthia, now disappointed with the system in the new environment and resenting herself for the mirage of the green pastures, returned to Brian and requested him to forgive her for her cowardly desertion.

Looking intently at her, Brian thought for a moment, "What if she abandons us again? When we needed her most, she left us without any regard for our human values. Is she really honest in her repentance?" Brushing aside all such nagging questions, he said, "Cynthia, we do not normally reconsider anybody who left us when we needed them the most."

Life is sometimes a best friend and always the worst foe to keep us on our toes! When we are uncertain or sure of something, life reverses our tendency and just prods us with a little more perseverance. Brian took a leaf from this lesson and spoke, "In your case, Cynthia, we think that we just should not repeat what you did to us," and afforded her another chance.

His consideration and open attitude toward her made her realize her folly. She developed in herself a new steadfast and conscious ally to Brian with her untiring dedication to the 'now-developed' work ethic and indomitable spirit for participation in local affairs. Brian justified his decision rather proudly to re-induct Cynthia and assigned the first task to survey the old buildings, and repair them on a war footing for housing the affected local population.

On the construction of the hospital building, Quinton gave thorough and deep consideration to the tensile strength of structures, floors, placement of machinery and gadgets, medical apparatus like x-ray, ECG, scanners, R&D laboratory, ICUs, operation theaters, and emergency wards, electrical and standby power supply systems. In all these exercises, Quinton meticulously involved Cynthia and the whole qualified medical and administrative staff on the payroll of the proposed hospital. The deliberations and discussions, sketches and draft revisions, designs, layouts, permutations and combinations of ideas, exchange of heated arguments, emotional outbursts - well, there was no end at all in the buzzing activity of the planning - an experience to live with. The hospital administration too poked its powerful nose now and then, exposing its creative lacuna!

Probably, the hospital construction would already have become buzzing with honey bees returning to their hive! With expert assistance from medical colleges and the best and most efficient medico team from the neighborhood hospitals, the construction of the four-story hospital was completed. At last, the little town saw, after six months, all of its efforts coming to fruition, adding one of the finest structural edifices to its public health gallery.

The advanced computer systems in every department, reception, bills/cash counters, in-house medical shops, ultra-modern technological instruments installed with proper and repeated trials taken, fully qualified and experienced medico staff employed, with other basic units as per the building layout was inaugurated by the Interim

President of the Hospital, Mr Brian, with a brand-new pair of scissors, cutting the pink silk ribbon band at the entrance with flower petals showering along the passage. The large wooden doors embodying the hand-carved Greek designs of the hospital Neigay Public Hospital & Health Services now opened its doors for general public welfare, with three ambulance vans in attendance outside the entrance.

Cynthia, proud to associate herself with Quinton in designing and constructing the hospital building, now happily rejoiced in her reverie to supersede Quinton and conduct herself in the role of Chief Executive Operations!

BRIAN WITH HIS SWEET HEART

"Now what?" a feeling of lacuna popped up, and Brian again became restless to conquer this agitation.

Brian spent some valuable time with his family and cherished their doting love and the congenial atmosphere which he tragically missed until now.

His granddaughter was an all-pervading spirit of joy bundled up in a sweet tiny girl. Natasha, the young girl in her late teens, playing with her same-age group of girls outside the cottage, quizzed herself looking at the old man, "Who was that?" With skin sagging from his chin, neck, and a little bit from his hands, Brian looked older than Natasha had seen him earlier as her young grandfather, and the passing years metamorphosed his physical frame so much that Natasha was unable to recognize him as her own 'grandpa'. Her curiosity overwhelmed her, and she spontaneously asked him, "Sir, who are you? Who all have come with you and anybody to play with me?"

Brian replied, "I am an old man." Feeling sad, he said, "Except me, nobody is here now to play with you."

He asked the girl what her name was and "Natasha," prompt was the response from the girl who very happily extended her reception to him. He called the little girl and queried what she was doing and where she was studying. Quite intense in their confabulation, they both were engrossed in various topics of discussion as though two mature and knowledgeable persons were talking with each other! *My granddaughter Natasha was really brilliant,* a satisfied pride slowly possessed him.

To hone her brilliance, Brian posed a riddle: "I have three children and each is older by four years than the younger child. How old is the middle child?" and explained how to solve the riddle.

Enjoying her innocence and her frolic spirits, Brian now disclosed who he was to Natasha. With a 'kangaroo' jump Natasha hugged him, crying ecstatically, and yelled, "Oh, my sweet grandpa." Their emotional outburst was a unique experience that grandparents would never afford to miss such exciting moments. He then bid her, "Go, now play with your friends and enjoy your game," so saying he bid the girl adieu.

Natasha fled the scene swiftly to join her grandmother, who was crouching on her sofa, leaning backward and gazing up.

"Grandma, Grandma," yelled the little Natasha with her sparkling and mischievous eyes while running from the patio.

"Oh, my sweet little darling. Tell me why you are running like this," Grandma asked.

"You know, I fooled grandpa," so ecstatic was Natasha. "How?" Grandma puzzled.

"Easy, Grandma. With both hands I kept at my back, I asked him, 'how many fingers open in my hand?' and showed my closed fingers in the other hand."

"Small children spontaneously adapt to happiness, sometimes erupting wildly like coastal waves and a while later mellowing with their mothers' quite naturally." her grandma thought aloud.

"So, you have now become a child again," Grandpa quizzed.

"Why again, you have left your work half done and come here to taunt me, and are you now a child!" beamed triumphant grandma. "You are right; I came here to see what you both do," Grandpa pulled himself with a sneering smile to his retreat and to continue his favorite pastime of newspaper reading and gradually visualizing the good days that he spent so endearingly with his family and children. He felt the goosebumps on his hands!

Taking a cue from him, Grandma closed her eyes to catch forty winks. She failed in her attempt and her memory unwound her school days' images. As a student in 5th grade, She now re-lived, her participation in sports, school annual day functions, elocution competitions, and other sponsored social events as well. In one of her school road patrol assignments, while assisting the traffic warden, she happened to sight an old man suddenly tottering in the busy traffic junction. Without blinking her eyelid for even a second, she daringly ran across to divert the speeding traffic to save the old man and ease up the traffic congestion. The little girl risked her life to help the old man while the onlookers gathered at the site to support her first aid to the victim. Not much untoward happened and the petite girl was remarkably swift to call an ambulance for emergency medical aid. With a precious alacrity and unhindered ability to respond to the crisis at such an early stage of her growth, she was then a shining star of the crowd!

Attired in a pink dress, hair in plaits neatly combed, clipped, and rolled both sides inward, Ramona, now a grandmother of the sweet little Natasha, entered the wedding hall like an imperious queen. Her blue eyes sparkling with a tinge of mischief and her half smile across her lips, she already was a charming girl, many young boys raising their eyebrows with anguished breath. As she was talking to one aunt on this side and with an uncle there, all young and old guests and visitors in the hall took turns to chat with her.

Just then, she saw a table laden with colorful gifts farthest in a corner, and picked up the large perfume bottle, and with a twinkling eye, she ran across spraying the perfume on the bride, groom, and all guests around the podium filling the room with fragrant scent. She ran like a rabbit with a girlish smile. Oh, what a scene full of surprise and a big melee!

There was another scene as the entire hall came in support of her pranks, "Oh, she is so sweet a girl! We all enjoyed some joyous time together amidst this wedding fervor." They asked her parents as to who she would marry and without any response, they left the wedding hall rather dissatisfied.

Brian, too, like his other youthful suitors, desired her hand in wedlock but lo, he was unsure of himself for such a worthy consideration and dejectedly shelved the idea forever.

Ramona now grew up to her age, a beautiful and tall lass in her twenties, grace fully embodied.

Magnetized by her captivating beauty, the local vagrant youth provoked her with their titillating remarks and comments to cause agony. They habitually treated all passers-by likewise, with little regard, most of all for their humanity. In one of the extreme situations, the vagabonds followed her, nagging, which annoyed her greatly. It was then that Ramona decided 'to teach a fitting lesson' to these bullies. She gathered some of the passers-by witnessing the scene and explained her intention.

She directly barged into the office of the local administration with her group where she met Brian in his chamber. Brian, in his meeting with some ward officers and laborer teams, was surprised to see Ramona stepping into his office and welcomed her enthusiastically. Explaining the continuous harassment of the roadside Romeos, she asked him if he could guide her to the proper authority or if he could himself help her tackle the nuisance of the thugs who ridiculed all passers-by, including old people, girls, and children of all ages. Brian, with all his ears to Ramona's purpose of her visit, orbited into space roving about this chance meeting with Ramona. "Sir, I am talking to you about the problem we have. You are drifting away and do not seem to care." Her admonition was gentle but pressed Brian back to his senses and promised to take 'essential steps' very soon.

He personally visited the site during the next two to three days and observed the scenario carefully to identify the whole gang, their style of working, pastimes, and habits. The local police, on his instructions, then initiated their action to detain them in the lock-up.

With a stern oral warning to either get their acts corrected or be sentenced under the Nuisance Act, all the ruffians were released solely in consideration of their current adolescent age and the need to nurture humanity for their future. That their act was 'a non-cognizable offense' was twisted to create a psychological effect on their social behavior. Brian had shown his logical influence and controlling power in the region.

Swift police action on local bullies brought back the town's calmness interwoven with its active life. Ramona and her friends were awestruck by Brian's protective action!

Ramona, accompanied by her friends and neighboring residents, met Brian in his office without an appointment to gratefully acknowledge his action and, thereby, his contribution to the honor and safety of local folks, especially women. As she was exiting his chambers, she turned to look at him and queried, "Why not join me this Sunday around 4.00 p.m. at Cafe Melodrama? We will have some 'special' and tasty delicacies with black coffee or fruit beverages," she offered to host. "Oh! That was pleasant," Brian responded mechanically without realizing how he responded so swiftly.

This invitation was most unexpected, and to join her for some ambrosial menu at one of the famous five-star cafes, 'Melodrama', on a Sunday evening, Brian imagined something more 'special' and he was unable to figure out what the 'special' was. This thought of meeting her pulsated his heart beat faster and out of its rhythm! He started mentally preparing how and what to talk interestingly to her and to retain her attention on him. He was overly cautious of himself not to irritate her on his topics of discussion, gait, and dialogue. What a change in the man who was a freak and recluse - Wow, every Brian in the world needs one Ramona, for sure!

His 'love at first sight' at a social function some years back and the recent meetings with her reignited his dormant desire for that girl's hand in wedlock, and at last, Angel Venus smiled at him! His love for Ramona now got a divine boost as well as a lively courtship from his heartthrob!

The youthful meetings wove natural dreams and intimacy, without the actual acquaintance of each other. With equal fervor and desire to see each other on one pretext or another, the truthful purpose of their meetings was never let out in the open between them. They both enjoyed their gibberish talks, laughed and smiled at each other, walked aimlessly along the mile-long promenade, and stayed together. The two cuckoo birds met at numerous local cafeterias and nearby coffee shops on different occasions.

Sometimes there were moments of emotional drift, and their egos swelled, causing them to stay away from each other. These emotional drifts brought them together again, like a flower bud with its innate fragrance, and like thorns, they added protection to the blooming love.

In the following spring, Brian and Ramona decided to enter into wedlock in the chapel after two years of courtship. The next Sunday saw them both happily embracing familial bond, exchanging rings that signified their wedding in the presence of a few select August and personal invitees. Their fresh faces radiated glowingly with their first kiss, which the cherry-red wine in guests' glasses reflected uncensored. That was indeed a simple celebration!

The newly married couple planned to go on their first honeymoon to Paris. With his obstructing social appointments, Brian and Ramona stayed locally, deferring their honeymoon tour. Both resumed their daily routines methodically long before the new marriage atmosphere had waned. Their dedication to their occupations spoke no more than that! Despite resentments and disappointments that brewed between them, they were together for some delightful moments, though not very frequently. Whenever opportunities knocked on their doors, they fully embraced them to be together like fresh lovebirds and continued to talk or discuss serious and nonsense topics under the sky with equal fervor.

In one of the early beautiful Friday mornings during breakfast, Ramona began to broach, "Brian, you are already deep in your work demands and schedules. Sometimes you come home so tired in the wee hours and without even noticing what is kept for you on the dining table, you munch and gulp without relishing your dinner."

"Our wedding just yesterday completed two months. Last night, I made your favorite sweet pudding, cognac, and your choice of delicacies, and they are still there. What's happening to you?"

Ramona was all loving and caring as a wife in her normal dialogue. Devoid of spousal maturity and stressed, Brian flared up at her, "Ramona, you are very sweet. Don't become a fishwife. I come home to regain composure from my work dictates. I did not eat what you made, and it was just that. So, do not make a mountain out of a molehill. Please ease up on yourself."

This was a bizarre moment at the breakfast table for which Ramona was totally unprepared. Instead of ironing out Brian's erratic and unreasonable outbursts on a pleasant Friday morning, she pulled herself into her own shell like a snail.

Every household accepted the first flare of the husband as an occupational hazard, and the wife generously overlooked that. The senior couples who aged with their experience in family relations advocated that this flaw was the primary root cause of divorces as the male ego was disproportionately pampered. They, however, admitted that they might have been wrong in some stray examples, as an exception!

The remedy suggested was open discussion, and the affected spouse got to gently wield the gavel. This is how, in the realm of the relationship, they generate their heirs to grow cohesively knitted like fabric in a responsible society.

That weekend, Brian fixed a beach resort for dinner and when he discussed his proposal with Ramona, she dismissed him, "Brian, you have a lot of work to do. Why waste time at a hotel dinner? In any case, I will not be coming with you for dinner." That was an indelible stamp of her still sulking over his outburst on the last Friday morning.

Pushed to a dead end, Brian returned to his normal self and said, "Ramona, not that I was angry with you because I wanted to. That was definitely not and would not be *me*."

In one of the recent flare-ups, Brian needed to intervene between two warring factions, one led by the most senior leader and the other by the young, qualified Turk, of his party cadres and pacify them, reminding them of their ultimate goal which would get vaporized with their fickle quarrels. What actually happened was that the young Carlson directed the elderly party worker, Rowan, to 'bring some of his party workers to the site and set his office up'. Rowan was upset with Carlson's indignant approach and retorted, "Mr Carlson, please update yourself with the party's primary working decorum and get your job done." Carlson considered this retort as defiance and yelled with scant regard at Rowan, "You all old people did not know what to do and needed to be sent back home." Rowan, in all his years of diligent functioning, was always ahead of his work dictates and never until now had such an unpleasant and intolerant rebuke outside his area of duty, especially from a new calf, Carlson.

The party work stalled and Rowan, with his loyal teammates, staged a walkout. Stunned by the turn of events, Carlson had no other choice but to report to Brian.

"The undue ruptures and bickering caused by power struggles left me with no solution beyond my maneuverability. And it just did not leave me with that. I felt no appetite, yet I saw the dining table neatly arranged by you and I ate what you had kept because chiefly I did not want you to feel slighted on that account. In any case, I am deeply sorry, I forgot our wedding day."

Brian attempted his marvelous assuage of Ramona, and he succeeded. Giving a jolt to Ramona, Brian swiftly pulled her close, eccentrically planting his kisses on both her cheeks. He got his sweet returns too.

Probably, the tussles and sweet nothings in the family are the finest sentimental texture to base for a congenial home! Such sweet harmony in the family always influences your social makeup toward national peace and prosperity. Their personal vibes are nestled in strong roots of respect and mutual understanding between them.

With the arrival of their first fortune girl kicking and cooing right from the second on landing cradle on this planet, the Brians' joy knew no bounds! The 'pinkie' baby was christened Natasha after the maternal great-grandmother and was all embodiment of her mother, including the most virtuous obstinacy of both grandmother and mother. They were elated just at her!

The whole of the women neighbors, who did not see the mother's crying and kicking in pain and anguish a little while earlier, were wiping their tears joyously to see the mother calm and dozing, and the baby now in the cradle looking up and rolling her eyes at the angels. For all those close friends and neighbors, it was a double joy for the mother and the baby as well.

The next 4-5 days saw the hyperactive relatives and friends thronging the new baby in her crib, ecstatic over her mumbling 'coos' and cries and sometimes prompting the baby to cry just to get a thrill of her baby voice. This pattern led to the neglect of their regular chores and schedules.

Natasha grew up adorning their family with her early baby pranks, typical characteristics of the first child. As is the universal custom, the first child was the dearest to the parents, family, friends, and neighborhood, who showered their love, spare time, fancy dress, and musical toys to spoil her to her heart's content. Natasha obviously enjoyed growing up with all their attention.

Brian, who earlier used to work long hours in the office, now sang a lullaby, holding the tender baby on his rough shoulders. Showing a crow here or mimicking a chirp, cuckoo, and cat, he was entertaining the child to his fullest potential. The truth was not clear whether Brian was himself enjoying his entertainment! Probably, not all parents get to realize this scenario. What was funny was when the father widened his eyes, aped like a monkey with his puffed mouth, hands holding both his ears to look like a hare, all in an attempt to amuse the baby. The child got accustomed to his tricks but did not relent in her ways to retain his love and attention. Quite a smart baby, she already knew how to attract boys!

A couple of years later, Ambrose, a robust boy, was born, and both parents and grandparents were proud to feel that this army soldier would tantalize their whole being and enrich their world in the footsteps of their disciplined beloved ancestors. He was no less than his elder sister in his pranks.

By turns, the grandparents and parents took children to picturesque nature: waterfalls, mountains, green plains, and gardens, letting them grow in its cradle, and were engrossed in watching both children play, cuddle, and fight for grandparents' hug or mother's lap. Both children vied together for simultaneous attention, pressed their cheeks on to gain that. Remarkably, focused!

Under their tutelage, Natasha and Ambrose learned to greet 'Good Morning', 'Welcome', and 'Thank you', quite early in their childhood and expressed short syllable dialogues, rural songs, watching TV programs, and from other neighborhood children. Slowly, they were taught to do some household chores and glided smoothly into doing tough tasks like purchases from the bazaar and booking prepaid cabs or other means of transport.

When Ramona's first great maternal uncle 'Sagora' visited them on a festival evening, both children's chorus welcomed him and kept him fully occupied with their antics, tales, and games. It was a joy a lot more for the uncle to seize his childhood and cherish with them!

Brian and Ramona were dutiful parents to the tender children Natasha and Ambrose, inculcating morals and a disciplined pattern of life in their growth. They explained with some examples of great historical warriors, curious human evolution, and civilization to imbibe in them a tendency to question and seek knowledge, besides instituting academic and sports interest facilities. Of course, national pride took precedence!

Ramona, with her already inherent sweet disposition and interpersonal skills, expanded her work beyond her family interests to enhance her spouse Brian's role in society and national interests. Brian, for his part, devoted some of his quality time to share with her and the children at the beginning of their new life.

They realized that *the basis of every living being is 'Family'* which is cohesively entwined as the soft fiber of universal love and care.

CHILDREN'S SCHOOL EDUCATION

Natasha, the first girl in the family, was now in her third grade at the co-ed school, and quite serious about her studies.

She took part in competitive sports, the school's annual day, and cultural functions. She was trained in a number of household services to make herself self-reliant in professions like plumbing, house cleaning, electrical work, and other daily essential services. Academically, she excelled by sharing her teachers' notes and homework assignments with her classmates and friends from other divisions.

She was popular within her friends' circle and was swarmed by her friends. "Mom, you know what happened in the class today? Our teacher conducted a class test in maths, and I came first with ten out of ten marks," excitedly Natasha said to her mom. Her mom hugged her, planted a kiss on her cheeks, gave her a bar of chocolate, and encouraged her, "Darling child, you are sweet and you have excellent talent to do even better. Go ahead."

Notably, every young child gets shaped strongly in her growth with abundant confidence from the parents' mere soft hugging and a small chocolate piece or bar. The academic performance bar, admission to an esteemed educational institution, and affluent status are all secondary dimensions, just citations on the child's primary confidence and outlook base.

Ambrose, their second son, growing robust with all his antics, was enrolled in the Montessori classes for training in reading, writing, expressive dialects, and sports. Waking the young tots from sleep and preparing them for their school routines, every mother felt it was easier to shift mountains and control civil riots.

Few mothers, however, admitted they too were typical of their children and of such lazy routines and behaviors, and they were always precedent examples for their children. So, why this grouse?

Unlike in the early days of schooling when the admission of a child was a matter of prime importance, the current system burns a hole in the economic stability of parents with its recurrent high cost of education. Often, affluent parents think, 'It is easier to possess a house in a posh locality or buy a new car with the latest technology'.

The sufferings and anguish of middle-class parents were inexplicably manifold. They could neither fulfill the genuine desire of their wards nor could they ever afford to sacrifice on any other front of their basics. Basic education is a luxury for the poor and a daily struggle for middle-class children!

TENTH WEDDING ANNIVERSARY

The day opened up and both Brian and Ramona, greeting each other, went about making breakfast - sandwiches with chicken, salad inserts, and a large mugful of coffee. As breakfast ended, Ramona reminded Brian, "Brian, today is our 10th wedding anniversary." She quizzed him, "How best can we plan to celebrate our anniversary together?"

"Oh! It just slipped from my mind. Obviously, I was sunk in work last night and when I came home, it was too late to do anything. OK, we will make up now," it was a matter-of-fact reply. "You are good at ideas and plans. Tell me about your plans," Brian prompted Ramona.

Though not very happy with Brian's casual response, Ramona suppressed her emotional disappointment in her mind. Contrary to her cheerful disposition, she softly replied, "Brian, it's all right; you need to work, and that, too, is very hard. But then, you have a family and there are some occasional festivities and social functions. You cannot afford to sacrifice your family's primary interests and welfare or forget them. You have hopefully prioritized your interests and needs henceforth."

"Now, we will plan a small get-together with our close kith and kin in the evening. You have a choice of venue or hotel and delicious à la carte?" She was remarkably shrewd to correct his lapse instantly and, at the same time, assuage his manly ego.

Brian was taken aback by the spontaneity of her barrage and then, her 'soft' caressing of his hands to ease himself. He was wondering about Ramona, 'how good she was' and 'was she a stateswoman like this from her birth'! Brian came out of his admiration and suggested to her as his participative gesture, "I am not good at organizing family functions or choosing the latest menu and trendy venue. You decide all that and arrange them as you feel is best, and I am with you all through your program to help and arrange our Anniversary, a grand and memorable celebration."

With select and restricted invitees, the evening program was organized in the town's north corner, at the reputed 'Paris by Night' a five-star hotel. The hotel manager, sensing the importance of their Anniversary Celebration, decorated its central hall with colorful lighting, banners and pendants inscribed with *'Happy 10th Wedding Anniversary to Ramona & Brian'*, dark and light-colored balloons attractively laid at the portico and entrance of the hall, and an orchestra troupe playing 'swing music' for the couple and invitees to dance on the floor.

The guests were dancing on the central podium to the tune of 'Mama Mia', 'I want you back', 'Lovely',

'What will I be', Que Sera Sera', and other favorite songs, all played by the musical minstrels chorused by the hotel troupe. Whether it was the chorus minstrels or a 'shot' of liquor on the rock, they never knew, but they enjoyed every moment of being on the podium and continued their sips while floating in space. This dance program spread gaiety and intimacy together, which some couples lost, and it brought their old love back between them.

Alongside was very pleasantly showcased the imported brands of premium quality liquors from sparkling champagne, apple wine, malt, scotch whiskey, and rum enticing the invitees. At another table lay neat large kegs and compact casks with soft beers especially for fastidiously selective women guests.

The farthest end of the lounge where a whole lot of Mexican, Italian, and Thai menus were decoratively set up, with starters of corn and tomato soups, steak, pasta dishes, omelets, and vegetarian curries made to order, their names displayed alongside the tables and gas stoves glowing with a thin flame to serve warm food forcefully drew your olfactory nerves and taste buds. In attendance were the highly professional bearers dressed impeccably in their golden uniforms behind each of the tables.

The guests gratefully acknowledged, "Ramona, it was a wonderful evening to be with you." That was definitely your achievement, and what we did not expect was your imperial reception to us to attend your wedding anniversary felicitation. "Both of you took strenuous effort to bring couples like us intimately together. We were a lot elated to experience gay abandonment." The guests bid customary adieu with greetings and gifts to the hosts post their dinner. Ramona and Brian exchanged their generous gesture and complimented with their token giveaway.

For Ramona and Brian, their jubilation still unabated; the celebration was a milestone in their wedding anniversary and a great triumph by itself to achieve its purpose, as most of the couples re-established closeness to each other that evening.

NATASHA'S SCHOOL PICNIC

In one of the dinner discussions, Natasha brought up her weekend picnic and entreated her parents to allow her to join the class picnic. Natasha was in her teens, and it was tentatively an educational picnic to make the students responsible for their social duties. Not to deter her in any way but to arouse her curiosity and to check her steadfast stand, Brian asked Natasha, "Darling, you have never spoken to us earlier! What is your school picnic program? Where are you all going to? How many of your classmates joined and why do you want to go on this picnic?"

"Dad, the picnic is organized by our school. There are three divisions of a total of 120 co-ed students. We will all be mobilized at the school stadium on the morning of Saturday at 8 a.m. We will then split into three omnibuses. With us are coming six female class teachers and two male PT instructors," replied Natasha. She handed a copy of the printed circular to her dad and addressed him, "Dad, you have all the details about our picnic, schedules, and programs in this circular. Read it as you please and discuss it with me in case you want to know anything that is left out."

"Dad, one last point: we may as well decline, and no need to oblige them," she was, for her age, very strong in psychology as she was reassuring her dad.

Pushed into a corner, Brian was unable to say his emphatic 'No' to her, and he was proud and elated as Natasha edged him in his tactical game effortlessly.

For the schoolchildren, the weekend always begins on Friday itself, even today. Joyously discussing and detailing their sports kit, musical instruments, plastic and fabric mat for gymnastics and yoga sessions, and clothing, socks, shoes, casual sandals, bed sheets, and woolen blankets, the students never find their list of items complete in their backpack, and there is always one item or another missing for inclusion.

Both teachers and parents found some solace in the short duration of their two-day picnic, as their food menu and schedules were precisely arranged.

More than their weekend picnic, it looked like their carry-all bags would have a jolly time getting strewn all over and giving a miss to their owners.

The students were assembled into six groups, 20 students per group and two groups for each bus, the school's identity batches hanging around their necks clearly displaying in big bold letters the students' names with contact details. Each group was assigned a class teacher and a list of students in her care and custody. All students were to report on time at the designated center without failure during morning breakfast, lunch, and night dinner. They all would be cleared to their beds for complete and sound sleep so that they would get ready the next morning to proceed with their picnic schedules.

On the first day of their picnic, the students were divided into different groups according to their interests in chosen games. The focus on students' interests weighed more on developing and honing their dormant talents to shine in later years rather than just passing time. Some students opted to play musical chairs, about 20 students participated in a 'reward and punishment' quizzing session, two pairs of students played ludo, and a group of students competed in a fugue composition of "Oh Maria" contrapuntally imitated by other students in their turns.

Post their lunch session, the supervisory teachers allowed a short cozy time, and students were obliged to be present by 2.00 p.m. to proceed on an evening trek up the terrain slopes. Each batch was closely and carefully monitored for safety. There were some slack, prolific moments as students, being growing teens, had their oozing energy, humor, and undomesticated spirits. Additionally, there was another specific reason: their parental control or regulation to keep vigil on them was absent, yet they remained cohesive and mature.

On the last evening of the picnic, Natasha and a few of her classmates were frenzied about trekking for a short distance and waywardly went on their adventure. The site was dark, filled with tall green foliage, and without a location map or directions. With their soiled shoes crushing and stamping dry leaves to squeak sounds, drizzling, and the emanating mud smell, dim daylight, the kids' trekking to a new unexplored area turned out to be a misery. Yet, *their spirits and attempts were laudable.*

Their absence in the camps created fear and disorder among teachers and students alike. With two PT instructors, four class teachers set out to trace Natasha and her classmates. One PT instructor with two class teachers went toward the southwest direction, and the other team went toward the northeast to search for the missing kids, both teams kept communication with each other. Their maturity rocked with repeated waves of giant anxiety about the safety of the missing students.

Natasha and her classmates found themselves huddled in fear, as they were unable to trace their return path to their camps. It was a scene of despair, and to dispel the dreaded atmosphere, they were idly chitchatting with one another.

Natasha then remembered her dad's golden rule, "In times of crisis, keep your composure, drink some water, and stay idle for a while. *At no time should panic control you. Gather your wits and carry on with your failures!* and you will get the desired solution."

Taking a deep breath, they all discussed and tried to remember their path and together ventured their return route cohesively. In some places, they missed their way due to diversion and then returned to the origin of the diversion point. As they continued their walk a little ahead, they paused to determine whether they were on the right course and then resumed their return along the correct path. As they progressed in their return trek, they faintly heard sounds floating in the air. Then they all paused en route to listen to the shrieking decibels of human voices and jumped abruptly in ecstasy. They identified their teachers' shrill tones echoing their names. Natasha and her classmates let out their breath in a sigh and shouted back to signal their whereabouts.

Hiking their way up to Natasha and her mates, the teachers reached them, hugged them, showering their love. The PT instructors explained how distressed they were and how much they all missed one another.

"Natasha, you made a good attempt. If you had informed us of your expedition, one of us would have joined to guide you all," chided the Senior and affable PT instructor, "and you would have gladly accomplished your purpose."

The reunion of kids with their respective parents after a two-day picnic was a much more ecstatic moment for the kids. They never got tired of narrating their adventures and felt bad that the picnic was short-lived.

They learned a lesson that their picnic was essentially a joint activity to stay together, an adventure for sharing risks and fear, and above all, grow mentally together with counsel from elders.

PUBLIC SERVICE & POLITICAL INVOLVEMENT

Recovering from the deep involvement in family routines and programs, Brian decided to plunge into his career and consider various options available to him. The options opened up encompassed big and already explored horizons like farming, trade, transport, and building.

He was not interested in any of these professions and was looking for something unique to pursue his passion. Nothing quite charmingly captivated him. He idly spent time roaming around the town, observing children and teenagers for their inspiring outbursts and activities, yet no clarity of his dream work dawned on him. Sometimes, life is sluggish!

An auto rickshaw with a folk song blaring out loud just sped past other vehicles, carts, and trucks along the buzzing avenues, and he looked at some billboards, some road signs, and stared far ahead until his eyesight strained.

As he continued his pace, he looked up at the sky intently and aimlessly. No, no, he is perfectly sane!

He returned to his abode to read some of his favorite classics, ranging from children's comics, epics, thrillers, and one or two spiritual books. The comic books with their colorful illustrations were a favorite pastime not only for him but also for older people.

On the contrary, the revered saints and scholars find the spiritual books - Psalms of the Holy Scripture, Old and New Testaments, Homer's 'Iliad' and the subsequent 'Odyssey' or similar works on sociology, the economy of dynamic civilizations - intensely rich in content but unable to be pursued for reading and grasping even at staggered intervals.

Brian still drew a blank on what he wanted to pursue further!

He discussed with Ramona, his friends, and well-known acquaintances his confusion in choosing a career. Their suggestions poured over all possible occupations involving trade, hotel, tourism, and government services like jobs in the army, air force, coastal guard, postal department, railways, and police. Every field offered abundant growth potential with its inherent drawbacks. Brian, from his earlier stint in book selling, building, and construction activities of the town's prestigious projects, *did not just want to relive his past* and so, brushed aside all such indicative suggestions. What he longed to do, something unique, was akin to a public utility service like a school teacher to satisfy himself. He decided to bide his time.

Days passed by, and one evening he attended by chance the pastor's sermon in the local church not so far off and yet not so close to his house. He was all ears, sparked by curiosity to find what the pastor was discoursing to the congregation. In his flow of sermon, the church father narrated various episodes on people's wayward pattern of living, squandering tendency, and *impatient urge to live for the present*, causing erosion in human values, and family bonds, with an overall impact on health and society.

He was goading the listeners to take a close and deep observation of all living beings and leafage with the natural forces of mountains and water bodies. "The reptiles, amphibians, or just for the sake of clarity, all quadrupeds subsisting for themselves on their own clan for food grow laterally. The hills, trees, and plants grow skyward, contrasting sunlight and rains falling on the earth inhabited by human beings."

"What use, then, are lightnings and thunders?" The parish explained that both help scatter their light and sound waves, creating magnetic fluctuations for our health in our daily lives. "This universe provides sunlight and rain, fire, wind, green vegetation, seas and rivers, land and underwater animals for our survival and welfare. Without Nature's bounty, we could never live on our own."

The pastor, absorbing the attention of community members, asked, "Why should I help or share my thoughts, my food, and my happiness with other humans? Are they reciprocating anything with me? They are so mean! What if they humiliate or disrespect my good intentions?"

He concluded, "We all live with doubts and irrelevant questions all through our lives. Like us, our friends and relations harbor such harmful mind ramblings. Ultimately, we contribute to the growth of lunatic asylums, shelters for both old age and orphaned children."

"Stop those harmful ideas then and there. The best way is, 'exchange your fears and doubts,' 'you may not get immediate clarity,' and sometimes 'your ego may get hurt,' 'still continue to meet your friends and relations,' the pastor besought the audience.

"It's difficult, still try to engage yourself in alleviating your self-doubts at the first instance and then the suffering of hapless people," nudged the wise pastor.

"You are what you wholly are, and your friends' negative criticism is like a raindrop in the sea, *useless*," the pastor was categorical! The pastor ended vividly picturizing how deeply the community welfare is beneficially intertwined in our lives.

Was it not a divine call that he attended the sermon which, in the first instance, he was so averse to that he did not care much about the religion and its patrons? It was a welcome turn for Brian as he drew some inspirational fillip and direction for an unknown destination.

Brian decided to go in for public service and enrolled himself as a primary party worker and volunteer in one of the social organizations owing allegiance to its parent political outfit, 'National Democratic Welfare and Progress – NDWF'.

He was spending most of his daytime in the local office, rendering sometimes useful services to the public like counseling and providing training to people on traffic discipline, banking and finance, local administration, enrollment of children in basic schooling and coaching them, encouraging arts and theater group performances, community festivals and celebrations, and other public activities.

The local populace was fascinated with his willingness to render immediate succor and his ability to provide clear direction to people on how and where they could get their work done, all free of cost. The townsfolk thronged to him for his kindness to assuage the feelings of those in troubled times and encouragement to those in need of healthcare. Brian was their beehive!

BRIAN AND JONAS NATHAN ENCOUNTER

Mr Jonas Nathan, the President of NDWF - National Democratic Welfare Front, a formidable opposition power to TSRU - The Social Reforms Union, was visiting the local town Neigay to institute the party's new offices in the region and strengthen the party workers' base of the rural units in and around that region. For his party workers, he was known as 'Joker Nathan'.

NDWF local party workers apprised Nathan about Brian's involvement in different public services as well as his growing reputation in the local area. On deliberation with local party workers, Nathan sent a party representative to call Brian for a brief meeting while inviting him to enroll himself in his party. Nathan clearly outlined the national objectives of the party and Brian's role, post-induction, in the regional outfit. Nathan, shrewd as President, promised Brian to help him rise in the organization, and Brian was expected to familiarize himself with the strengths and weaknesses of the party cadres, with suggestions to improve the party's performance and reputation.

The local people and media became excited about Brian's new identity in their favorite political party. In celebration, they all took out a jubilant procession through the residential and market areas of the town, and people thronged to witness the gaiety.

The deeper he plunged into public service, the less he was able to associate with and care for his family, sacrifices inevitably inherent.

The new areas of interest then unfolded to shape his constructive imagination and test his mettle. His hard work and overflowing interest in public involvement scaled in his party ranks, winning a majority in the recently held regional elections. He was the people's man and a natural choice for the Office of the Regional Secretary *Tanjo*, which had administrative jurisdiction over his native town Neigay.

His social stature grew steadily. The people who were happy to get his assistance and help had directly contributed to his party's growth too. His green-eyed rivals sprout like weeds with those unsatisfied people, perversely dreaming of his early downfall. That was indeed his growth as well as the first phase of a likely pitfall; he knew for sure that he was both jubilant and sad!

Abruptly tossed from his sleep, Brian rose from his bed and switched on the electric kettle for his hot cup of black coffee. Still in his night attire and with the coffee mug in his hand, he picked up the newspaper 'The Glorious Morning'. As he was flipping through, a news item on the fourth page attracted his attention. The regional outfit of the opposition party TSRU - The Social Reforms Union - in alliance with some disgruntled members from his party was organizing agitation on the high prices of essential edible stock, oil, and fuel, the much alleged anti-people administrative policies, and the ineffective police force which caused deteriorated law and order in the region.

While going through the news in its full coverage, his mind dwelled on the "disgruntled members" and he knew instantly that every home had at least one inseparable and inherent fuliginous seed. While trying to figure out the disgruntled members to contain the spread of revolt within the party, he succeeded in precisely narrowing down the vandals behind this chaos.

Brian initiated administrative steps to revamp the slack administration by relocating efficient and experienced senior officers and transferring all inept staff beyond the disturbed region. He regrouped select party office bearers to ensure the smooth flow of trade and commerce through streamlined and increased frequency of transportation. Besides, he summoned the press and media with a TV crew to propagate the government's policies and actions and to reiterate his government's assurances in constant updates for the public at large.

The - TSRU - The Social Reforms Union - members and disgruntled party cadre, with socially tagged unsocial elements, caused terror for the safety of common folks, damage to public edifices, health and research institutions, and food-stock warehouses. The erupting social unrest created psychological fear of life insecurity. This fearsome situation confounded the townsfolk and restricted their social and economic movements within the confines of their homes. This catastrophic impact plummeted the state's economy with rising demands for essential supplies.

But life is not all that rosy! Red, pink, and white roses, with thorns and contrasting green leaves, spread their original fragrance and natural beauty.

Everywhere all negative elements got an unnecessary boost, the irony of it is that it originated from their own homes! The forces outside the state funneled the arson, making the rescue of many innocent people and children entrapped a tedious task, and the local law and order was sabotaged to a mere passive witness.

Mr Jonas Nathan, the President of the National Democratic Welfare Front, was enraged with all the happenings in his state and convened an emergency video meeting. Categorically castigated for his inept administration of the government and the state party wing, Brian was asked to step down. Then, to contain the staring unhappiness in the party cadre, Nathan brought George from the party's HQ office to take the top position in place of Brian.

Did replacing Brian from his office restore peace and normal life in the state?

George, a novice in politics and administration but a powerful and trusted aide of the president, took his time to assess the situation. After assuming office, he proclaimed a law banning public gatherings. With that, George imposed a curb on the assembly of all prominent people during the day except for religious and wedding purposes. Not content with that, George sanctioned the police with the due powers to take action for the lock-up of accused and suspects. Other savage methods comprising water cannons, baton-wielding, and shooting on-site to disperse the vandals were adopted.

For complete control of local governance and party members, he replaced his dependable friends in select positions. As a last resort, imminent imprisonment of the vandals without court trials for all the civil unrest and sabotage of properties was decreed. The general public though voted the party to power for its welfare policies and promise of efficient governance and observed the party's mishandling of public affairs.

The large unruly elements of society, supported by the disgruntled party members, protested in unison against such totalitarian control. The spillage of broken glass bottles, burnt shoes, footwear, and tires, torn cloth rags, their sparks flying in the air, crushed and rotten green vegetables, dry leaves, sauces, and eggs, hot and twisted iron bars, and crumbled plastic wares photo-flashed faint double images of gory ghosts floating over that scenic spot!

Brian knew that such preventive steps would amortize the people's faith in the governance and foresaw a switch of their favorable support which the party until now enjoyed. The discontent popped its head, as envisaged by Brian, deflecting a gradual shift of their faith and loyalty from the party. This obviously forebodes a slump of the ruling NDWF's influence and with a possible increase in the opposition party TSRU's chance to reign in.

"How do I respond to the current chaos?" Brian was sad to ask himself. He assembled all his friends and faithful well-wishers for an urgent meeting. While discussing the economic damages sustained, he had deployed some of his influential aides to get all common folks released from the prison. At the end of the convention, he had presented before them his plan to speak to the Party President Mr Nathan in an attempt to improve the chaos-ridden situation.

His friends, well-wishers, and followers did not approve of Brian's suggestion of approaching the President of NDWF, Mr Nathan. They all had voraciously put forward a replacement proposal which would be the reinstatement of Brian. After updating the current state of affairs, Brian suggested Nathan either replace George with a more capable party leader or reinstate himself to the position. This arrangement would facilitate boosting the party's sagging image and reputation and, to a great extent, soothe the antagonized public.

Mr Nathan, assessing the party's diminishing rank in the state, conceded Brian to regain his position. A strategic ploy and a small solace, indeed!

Loyalty, it is always true, *brews unhappiness.* Its spirit and strength are indomitable. You have just one choice, 'comply fully with it or you never recover from its punishment!'

His capable administrative staff, led by Brian, went about the task at hand of assessing the extensive damages that the recent vandalism had caused to the buildings and ruined public utilities such as roadways, parks, and schools.

Brian employed an additional labor team to clean the road, collect all broken and dirty spills of garbage, and pave the road for the smooth movement of people and merchandise. These relief measures helped people move about, easing the tense situation. The townsfolk returned to their daily activities, buying their choice wares, meeting friends, and spending time with close relatives and other social activities.

From education to traditions and customs, the man is taught only the damage control modes and preventive techniques. Brian was melancholy to query, *"Why then is he not pushed in to tap that potential of his foresight conducive to harmony."* No erudite scholars and wise statesmen ever saw their minds on this muddle.

Their confidence in Brian hitherto, dented as a result of recent social disturbance in the town. The revival of the town's hegemonic life cemented their faith in his leadership skills! Bravo, the town's people had a leader now!

Assembling all the citizens at the council hall, Brian presented before them his sketch of revival activities to be taken up in the next two to three years for the town's progress. He invited them for free counseling and directions. His mere idea was not to take them into confidence alone but to gradually involve them as a team with their equitable participation in the local governance. That involvement would create awareness of their whole responsibility toward the state. It seemed a good idea and the townsfolk instantly responded.

"My dear friends, some of you will be disappointed with me for not getting the recognition due to your mettle and ability and a chance to contribute. Do not get crestfallen. We have many openings to fill with able and talented people. Out of all the vacant positions, police, Public Distribution, local administration, and Revenue are featured in our immediate consideration."

All experienced senior people are provided with the opportunity to utilize their knowledge in the innovative generation methods of public funds, and fair collection and prioritize their distribution on projects and local administration.

All physically able youth will be drafted into the police to maintain law and order. For their patrol and effective discharge of their duties in the sustenance of absolute peace, they will be provided with all utilities and facilities at their disposal, in addition to attending to emergencies.

"Next are the important portfolios of Education, Construction, and distribution of public utilities like electricity, water, etc. All eligible children will be mandatory schooled, and the Governor will manage and update their curricula, institutions, and educational policy.

Similarly, in construction and water works, all unemployed youth and middle-aged individuals up to 35 years old will be trained in such high physical activities of the town.

"It is most important that you all understand and remember well that in your work, you will face many problems with your colleagues, superiors, and bosses. Quite often, external influences affect material transportation, or sometimes your family members' sickness or health problems may add one or two obstacles. Please step forward to your immediate boss or supervisors without hesitation and discuss to find a practical solution to your problem. The more you do your work well and without interruption for the benefit of society, and that includes your welfare too, you prosper with your health and happiness."

Thus, all fields were filled in with the required expertise and every department was streamlined at the first instance to put into a smooth functioning pedestal. All departments were constantly monitored under the alert supervision of Brian, who moved inconspicuously from one place to another. While meticulously elevating the star performers with due recognition and more responsibilities, their morals were softly encouraged lucratively. In short, this level of competitive involvement in their jobs pressed under-performers to vie and better their performance. Sometimes those who were under observation until now were shifted to suit their abilities for better performance. The motto was 'best performance'.

Public Distribution, until now a large central body infested with slack and demoralized garb up to its base roots, was split into small units. Each unit was tasked with a separate domain like procurement, storage, transport, and distribution to serve the local distribution system without any blotch. Each unit head of this system was reporting to the local administration with transparent and specific guidelines on supply replenishment, distribution, and stock at the depot.

Construction activities were also very carefully monitored from the initial stages of sampling, procurement, storage of quality material, supervision of the proper concrete mixing ratio in compliance with structural specifications, distribution at every site, laborers' working time and efficiency, and prompt wage disbursal. The competent local authority always enforced vigilant control of men and materials. He was required to be present fortnightly at the task committee for transparent updates.

The interest levels peaked, and a sense of competition surged, with incomparably the best performance witnessed in every sphere, eclipsing their own previous best-preceding models.

Capitalizing on his position as head of the State administration and the state unit of his party, Brian aspired to draft a National Program. Time was not then ripe for Brian, with Nathan orchestrating strings of his party's discordant notes. Besides, what Brian had in mind on the National Program was a very wide framework to be adopted on members' consensus. The clarity and direction were spelled about people's rights to practice their faith in their culture, religion, and social norms. The existing hazy cultural, linguistic, and religious policies aggravated the attitudinal differences of the population and hence, the draft plan gave a big and serious headache to Nathan and his zealots for their own stay.

A few presentations of the draft policies outlined by the policy framework committee were rejected as many elected representatives and their followers found one or another partisan conflict. They strongly voiced inadequate consideration of their people's rights and representation. All such rejected policies were sent back for reconsideration.

The National Policy, as an overall and adjunct document to the already existing policy, would be considered not only from the existing rights and safety of every citizen but also from the future perspective of their economic growth and health.

This should be strengthened by creating opportunities for additional infrastructure for free and fair movement of merchandise, a transport network, and fearless movement of the population with a competent law-enforcing system to curb and punish all usurping activities besides enforcing the safety of women and elderly people.

The opposition members saw this as a ruse to strengthen and expand the ruling party's operations while the policy imposed an inconspicuous check on their expansion activities. Calling for an increase in construction activities in dams, bridges, and natural water bodies across all regions to cater to their party cadres' interests, they staged non-participation in the convention.

Nathan, being the president, intercepted to seize all powers and commanded the party to work with the police to control untoward tendencies. This high-handed preventive action, though quelled the disquietude, churned some unhappy waves in the party.

On different public platforms, they accused and traded charges with Brian and his team: "Brian was quiet about our National Policy until now as a disciplined member. Now he is abruptly amending the policy. Why? We challenge Brian on this podium to meet us and explain to the nation his motive." The comprehensive nationwide media propaganda with vested interests for their mileage joined in their scathing attack on the National Policy.

Brian and his team deployed numerous print media to reach the ultimate beneficiaries. The colorfully printed pamphlets explaining the policy to the general public were distributed on a door-to-door level supported by full-size advertisements in the national press to keep the large audience abreast.

"We do not consider the opposition's negative views and suggestions," Brian's firm voice blared in all audio programs. "We stay and will continue to remain with our integrity until we achieve the ultimate goal of our people's welfare."

"The existing policies create lopsided avenues to vested interests for growth in society. The low cadre people are exploited in connivance with these provisions. Left with no alternative, the opposition parties make loud and empty calls to stage a theatrical performance. We accept our dear opposition parties' invitation to meet on public platforms and I proclaim that the proposed amendments in the coming session are designed to fill the lacunae and to accentuate citizens' rights and public participation."

It was a soft yet strong retort played intermittently to pique the public's curiosity and attention on "What is Brian's reaction" or "How Brian responded" against the loud and aggressive calls from the opposition.

Much against their move to stall the activities on the inclusion of a wider spectrum of the amendment in the National Policy, Brian, with rock-solid support from his party members, swayed their policy for adoption. The members' vociferous debate, emotional outbursts flaring up, and the thunderous melee in the assembly came out to the public's notice with a big question, "Did we elect them? Are they representing us?"

Now that the society's interwoven texture is coming under threat and disruption, Brian amalgamated his party members and police team to assuage the situation. Nathan took stock of Brian's role and his expanded activities in public policy on the national level and considered him as a serious and growing threat to his own position. "Would Brian upscale himself to Numero Uno rank in the party?" psychic fear chilled up his spine. Nathan felt his innate urge to retain his supreme position in the party and an impending need to block Brian's growing popularity and, with that, end his political rise.

George, the only available protégé, was pitted against his arch-rival Brian to check and cause a 'go-slow' phase of Brian's program. This slow phase, the president hoped, would cause flutters and dissatisfaction among his opponent's fans and followers and, in a way, would entrench Nathan's tentacles in their absolute power without much of a waning of the party's image at the grassroots level. The political commotion bade logic a befitting farewell.

As all programs and activities seeped with tardiness in their phase of implementation, Brian was befuddled and profoundly irritated at the snail's pace. He couldn't endure the delay and summoned meetings as often as he felt necessary with his party workers to ascertain the reason therefor. Lastly, Brian reached the work site and spoke to some labor teams. This meeting gave a graphic picture of the pending disbursement of basic labor wages, discontinuance of canteen facilities, and extended working schedules without equal compensation, which resulted in mass absenteeism, non-cooperation, and go-slow motion from their co-workers and inordinate delay from the supportive utilities departments.

Brian's rage crossed all barriers and dashed to Nathan's office to talk to him about why such problems were created. Mr Nathan, on his part, adopting a tactical game, delayed his meeting ostensibly due to his preoccupation with administration and party work. Nathan then messaged Brian that he would revert shortly with his appointment for 'Mr Brian' to meet him. The style of addressing 'Mr' at the end of the short message alienated Brian from the intimate wavelength with Nathan. Brian tragically continued to wait with 'hope against hope' for the promised appointment with Nathan to materialize.

At last, Brian realized that time was pushing him to take drastic measures to replace all disturbing elements. Giving careful thought to the modus operandi, Brian found himself plotting identically along the lines of his party president's earlier thoughts. For a moment, he felt good to ask himself, "Why not take up the party presidency? By doing so, I will be able to speed up the drafting of policies and the implementation of welfare projects without much undue delay. If any external troubles and obstacles seep in to block the projects, I, as the President of the party, am well-equipped and better placed to swiftly obliterate all those obstacles."

A sense of realization to aptly project himself as the National Leader of NDWF taunted him. At first, Brian wasn't averse to the idea at all, and viewing the stagnation of policy implementation, Brian thought to give an all-out try for his idea, gauge the outcome and sentiments of the public, and held preliminary discussions with some of his friends, well-wishers, and dependable allies in the party.

With uniform approval from all party ranks and files, Brian called in all media players in the country for a high tea meeting in which he unfolded his plan of a national-level action as a stunner. Expectedly, frenzied ecstasy with the contrastingly violent tempers and agitation erupted sky-high.

Nathan, now pushed into a corner by the growing dissent and recent developments, summoned Brian for an immediate meeting to discuss all the problems. Nathan, on his hotline, spoke to Brian, "Brian, some grave lapses took place under my own plan, and I know this caused a great deal of anguish and disrespect to you. To make amends," Nathan further continued, "Brian, you are appointed as the Governor of the Western Province, in addition to being the Vice President of our party."

Brian thought, 'That's quite a good temptation' and said, "Sir, I am elated with your offer."

"Specifically at your instance, our top-ranked party leaders engage to belittle and disgrace me on a number of occasions and at various public platforms."

"Often you are tacitly encouraging them in such activities. What is more bothering me is how our party would treat the general public. I am unable to imagine the impact."

"I and all party workers in my unit continue to contribute to the party's growth and image. As a reward, what we get from you is ill-treatment always. This is not acceptable to me," replying thus, Brian concluded, "My apologies, Sir, to decline your magnanimous offer," and suggested Nathan step down in the interests of the party.

Furious with Brian, Nathan was unable to contain the damage any further. In a fit of rage, Nathan sacked Brian from the primary membership of the party and took a sequence of actions against all his loyal supportive members. "What you sow, you reap." Nathan got his own choice of 'payback' from Brian.

Now freed from the party's shackles, Brian felt elated with his free time.

AN ODE TO ZURICH

For Brian and Ramona, it was one of their happy family times, when Natasha and Ambrose joined them in their Sunday lunch, as otherwise family members took lunch individually at the dining table when hunger banged its head. Ramona noted, "It was always good to assemble at the dining table at least on Sunday and eat together. Mercy to you, Lord," she was so grateful.

Both their children animatedly started the topics of that day's interesting soccer, TV episodes, of their neighbors' escapades and at last, centered on the neighbors' visit to England in the forthcoming Xmas and New Year holidays. They both chorused, "Except for local areas and our school excursions, we did not go anywhere."

"Hallelujah, Our children are quite creative and enthusiastic," Ramona voiced excitedly. "We have school vacation for nine to ten days this Christmas season. We too would like to go and see the outside world at least a little for some days, and our children need to meet different people, their rich cultures, experience the outdoor scenery," Ramona told Brian, supporting their children.

"Natasha and you, Ambrose, if you have any idea where you both would like to go and see around, get some details about the place. We will plan now something for a short visit," a very wise Ramona said in her tactic way of occupying children and taking some private time to talk to her husband, Brian.

"Brian," began Ramona, "our children's desire is quite normal," and it is our duty to fulfill that small desire of our children. You are submerged neck-deep in your profession, and I, too, need a change of scene. Let's all go out for a week somewhere in Europe like Zurich, Amsterdam, Venice, or Florence." More than her children, Ramona was exhilarated to discuss this topic.

Passively listening to Ramona all through her talk, "Honestly, I do not think it is possible at this moment. Yet, you are right; we need a change of place and fresh air. This is also the right time for children to go outside their school and see different places and people."

Just then, the trio - rugged David, his wife Caroline, and their petite daughter, Grace from Georgia, sojourned at Caroline's cousin Ramona's during the Christmas advent, showcasing their pompous lifestyle far away from their homeland. Their visit was a bolt from the blue and was out of sync with their Western culture, which always adhered to the trend of calling on friends and relatives by prior appointments and traditional invitations.

With a customary reception and exchanges, they settled cozily and reminisced about their childhood.

Probably, in their middle-aged lives, when the household economy and social status grabbed all of their concentration, their lives did not afford time to live for the present.

At last, they sat just before their sumptuous luncheon. Decorated with a variety of enticing Mexican, Continental, and Thai menus. With the arousal of their mouth-watering senses, the husband and wife opted to take a circular glance with a polished smile. "Oh, this delicacy is excellent, 'good varieties', the dinner arrangement is awesome," and then filled their plates with a little of each dish to make it a single-course menu. The parents politely guided their daughter (of course, quite grown up, well-educated, and independent) to go easy on her helpings, "like us!" They pretended that climate change and different food seasoning might not be suitable for them. All maternal and paternal niblings and peblings are just chips off the same block!

A stark contrast in oriental culture needed to be highlighted. In the Far East nations, visits were spontaneous and always uninvited In every household, people from relations, neighborhoods, and friends thronged and cheerfully mingled with one another, spreading an air of total abandonment of unnecessary formalities.

It was not only queer but unheard of, within relations and genuine friends' circle, to take prior appointments or to be invited for our visit to our own relations and friends. Hypocrisy is not uncommon here too!

Fully sunk in pretensions, the trend in Western civilization to visit relations and friends was chiefly by prior appointment, even for family get-togethers and functions, and in other cases, strictly by invitation.

Relieved from the guests late in the evening, Ramona and Brian got together to work on their plan. "OK, Ramona, now listen carefully, we cannot go for a long vacation. Plan for a five-day stay in your chosen location with to and return flights taking just a day, and we will all be away for a total of seven days. Give me your final program, and I will make arrangements for our tour, hotel accommodation, and local transportation bookings."

Ramona, Natasha, and Ambrose were confused, unable to choose any one particular exotic location as they found all cities irresistibly attractive, offering them a lot of recreational activities like ice-skating rings, Dolder Sports in Zurich, Canal House, Van Gogh art gallery, Amsterdam History Museum, Rembrandt House Museum, and Windmills in Amsterdam, in addition to captivating natural scenery. After studying the availability of comfortable hotel rooms and flights, they chose Zurich for all of their four days' recreation.

In Zurich, Swiss Alps by day 1, Opera House and Prime Tower at night on day 2, Felsenegg Cable

Car and Ferry Ride on day 3, and the Swiss Federal Institute of Technology Zurich [Eidgenössische Technische Hochschule Zurich] on their last day, which composed their whole itinerary plan.

Brian, Ramona, and their two children, with two large suitcases lugging on caster wheels, one backpack stuffed with travel documents, a camera, and, importantly, all other items for their itinerary, boarded their 'Intercontinental Air', an ultra-huge recliner flight with free space, impeccably friendly aircrew, and in-flight meal service. This was a unique experience for these first-time air travelers.

What is more, aircraft pilots' efficient maneuvering prompted the children to raise doubts, "Dad, why are we still on the ground?" By then, the flight was well on its course above thirty thousand feet elevation.

In Zurich, Natasha and Ambrose saw a white-bearded, red-suited, and joyous Santa Claus gliding with mounts of attractive packages for distributing to all nice boys and girls in the streets, malls, theaters, and gardens with Xmas and New Year's greetings and goodwill messages all across.

While in the Alps, Natasha and Ambrose wished to try ice-skating, but due to a lack of equipment and adequate training in the sport, they were denied. They walked around the skating arena, discussed with the players, felt the skateboards and equipment, and collected souvenirs.

On the second day, their journey in the cable car was an astonishingly breathtaking experience, while the ferry ride with the cool breeze splashing water in their faces was a blissful tickle, which they preserved to cherish frequently and share with their schoolmates and other friends.

On New Year's Eve, after their visit to ETH, Zurich, they all melodiously chorused the carols at the local church. When they returned, complete and eerie darkness covered their hotel, and at the first musical chime of the large bell in the town hall, shouts and joyous waves of feelings floated in the air. The occupants, known and unknown, until now aloof and reserved, all exchanged 'Happy New Year' freely, with hugs, handshakes, and a peg of their choice Champagne. For Ramona and the kids, it was all fun, and they proceeded to their à la carte dinner.

"Ambrose and Natasha, it's time now for all of us to get some small sleep and get refreshed. We need to rush in the morning to catch our return flight during the day," so saying, Brian packed them into their beds. Christmas and New Year still lingered in their minds. Brian, with Ramona, Ambrose, and Natasha, was reliving their joy in their haven, Zurich, and they felt a tinge of sadness as all the new and happy moments were coming to an end.

The advent of the New Year and the sweet memories of their pleasure trip to Zurich were lingering afresh. Ramona took specific note that all such sweet and memorable experiences faded with the passage of time, while the harsh and bitter sufferings were indelibly etched in our memory (even our own memory is sadistic to portray the most unwanted situations!) throughout our life.

BIRTH OF A NEW POLITICAL PARTY

Brian's parting from the parental body of the party spread like wildfire with good coverage and people's faith in him popped its head an inch more.

With the birth of the new political party 'Common Welfare and Progress of our Nation (CWPN)', Brian moved his national plans and programs with furious fervor, pushing all of his army of men, party cadres, and the general public into every nook and corner as though they all were running in the Olympics in the final leg of the race with Brian.

Ignorant and tardy staff, as is everywhere, neglected to keep up with changing times and stalled all-round growth to a large extent. His one-man show was handicapped everywhere to streamline and oversee his new party's infantile activities.

It was at this juncture that his intuition to bring in a second-in-command person to control and coordinate with party workers at every level swiftly and smoothly pushed him to action. Brian was looking for an able person, through party files and ranks as well as through some influential friends, to associate with people all around.

The second-in-command, he very clearly visualized, preferably a feminine gender, justifying and in full support of his National policy for equal participation and who would be able to garner people's support. While holding her fort with her fans and followers in its rock-solid strength, she should, at the same time, be accessible to both her cadres and the general public. Yes, only that way we should achieve our purpose, he thought with a nod of his head.

While the search was on, he saw that his lower cadre labor wing reverberated with enthusiasm at the high level and work was going on as if one of their best friends would scale up to that position.

In one of the all-women social conferences, Ramona was invited to speak on the current tendency of family disintegration in the pursuit and fulfillment of economic freedom and stability. This invitation was a big jolt to Ramona, as she never had the opportunity to foresee such a situation.

Many women spoke elaborately on the impact of family disintegration, failing to touch the core and remedy, Ramona observed. At the end of the conference, Ramona brought the audience's attention to current and diverse social entertainment activities: restaurants, bars and parlors, casinos and electronic game centers, theaters, and TV occupying the spare time of both men and women. "Such wayward spending got to be curtailed. We would educate our family members on the importance of a cohesive family unit and its benefits in the long run," she concluded.

As a first step, she introduced in her own home a series of preventive courses.

MOTHER'S LESSONS TO NATASHA AND AMBROSE

Ramona had both Natasha and Ambrose seated along with Brian in the living room and started to tell them, "You both are growing up and this is a very ripe time for us to teach important life principles and good habits for your growth. Periodically, you will continue to learn one new skill, develop and practice it to perfection, alongside your school lessons."

"I've put up a small list on the eastern wall of our living room. This list is only for the first six months, and a new list will replace it. So, try to get an idea of physical activities and scores of new skills outside your academic subjects, from which you will pick up one that stirs your interest to learn and specialize later."

1. You will develop firstly your own self-respect uncompromisingly. Give respect to demand your respect.

2. Reach and connect to meaningful friends adaptable to your caliber. Once you have adopted and developed a friend for all times, stand by him in all his ups and downs.

3. Your moral values are like your breath. You need to regulate and retain them constantly.

   No foul language. Conduct yourself bravely. Your message is always clear and very direct to the point.

4. Complete your school assignments before your dinner and revise them before you retire to bed.

5. Between April and June this year, you will learn two new skills, the first being swimming and the other skipping rope.

   The second skill you would choose from any area that would absorb your interest and talent.

   I learned recently a few new words in a totally different language that helped me communicate effectively with my clientele.

The two Japanese words are:

"Uketamo" - 'I accept with my open heart'.

With repeat use of this phrase, you would identify the areas falling beyond your scope of improvement, and it would help you focus your efforts where you need to.

"Arigato" - 'Thank you'.

   With daily usage practice, you would develop deep meaning with its verbal expression. As you would converse in the local lingo, it would endear you to all your friends and relatives.

6. Do not waste your food. Be grateful and gracious.

"Continual learning is actually your living, like good sleeping. Remember, you cannot afford to slack. If you still wish to go easy on your schedules, be ready to sacrifice your chances of good living and sound sleep."

Natasha and Ambrose were aghast, "Oh, Mom, we do not want to go by your wish. We have our own games and pastime interests," both distastefully conjured.

"And one important point: You have no choice but to readjust the above agenda to suit your mood." Ramona left no room for the audience!

"Oh, this is like military," Brian implored, "Ramona, please be a little considerate to our children and a little more to me too. We all are human beings."

"Once you get accustomed to going by relaxation or ease of attitude, your mind becomes a slave to it," Ramona admonished Brian, and that was more than a pointer to Brian, too, besides both children.

"Enough, and we end this discussion," the mother rather unwillingly closed the topic.

Ramona, after seeing her children off to their rooms, called Brian and discussed with him the status of his party affairs and his future course of action. Brian mentioned the necessity of a second-in-command person to support his party's organizational and administrative activities. He explained that most of his cadre lacked public relations or administrative ability.

CAROLINE, RAMONA'S BEST FRIEND!

The day dawned with so many household errands and demands. More from Ramona and the children, being what they were, had occupied his constant attention. The children were fond of their dad and took his time with their antics and games. This was often a pleasant pastime for Brian, too, upsetting his cool 'pet dad' composure. Brian was unable to concentrate on his work. Sometimes, he felt he neglected his primary 'Self' for days together and was just living a skeletal.

"Ramona, you are doing a good job efficiently managing your family, kids, and your profession. I don't know how you are able to cope so dexterously. Why not share some of your creative techniques to help me with my work too," mellowed Brian in his dictating self.

With a fixed gaze on Brian, Ramona was in her elemental self to quiz him, "Tell me clearly how you want me to help you in your work?" Quite glad in her swift and adept retort, Brian said, "No, no, you are mistaken. I manage well with my schedule and that's not the problem at all." To this, Ramona replied, "Brian, we have been together for over two decades, and you do not need to cajole or engage in pep talk." Happy with the turn-out of this escapade, Brian elaborated to her on all his failed attempts to prop up the party and the growing job pressure and responsibilities that he was singularly unable to attend.

Ramona, pondering for a minute, said that one of her able confidants would meet him in the next few days and that the candidate would rise well above his organizational needs.

Ramona, with her earnest desire to help Brian in his political office, brought in one of her able college mates, Caroline, with a master's in political science as her major. Standing at five feet seven inches tall, slim, with curly hair rolled up behind her neck, enchantingly attractive, and in her thirties, Caroline had all passers-by riveted to her.

On her first meeting, she was pleasant and naive with her political exposure but responded boldly, "Sir, with my current administrative job, I am quite positive I can add to your reputation as the 'People's best friend,'" and she clinched the job offer.

Caroline adeptly glided well into her new job with all her knowledge and talent.

CAROLINE'S INDUCTION

Brian added some intensive training dimensions with repeated and systematic on-the-job performances and frequent rotations to different working situations to complete the formal induction of Caroline into his new party. This exercise was to help her acquire expertise in the current state of affairs, projecting herself as the party's Public Relations Manager and being able to face untoward situations on her own.

Caroline, in one of her camps at the adjoining hamlets, visited each household, introduced as a representative of CWPN, tried to find out, "You might have gone through some hurdles in procuring your daily edible items like bread, eggs, oil, etc., from the public distribution store, or public transportation, and public services. Please speak freely to me about what you would like me to do to mitigate your sufferings and improve your welfare." She was forthright and open in her exchange of views and actions, "We will try to reduce the hardship soon." As a start-up exposure of her public interaction, she projected herself as an able and supportive cadre from CWPN.

While she was on her job, Brian steadily added to keep her on her toes for periodic updates and feedback on his party members' performance and hassles. This rigorous training imbued the cat's agility in her to maneuver the intra-party bickering, reshuffling of cadres within the regions, and the opposition's horse-trading tactics.

That Caroline was naturally shrewd and able was way beyond our doubt, but the sinuous ways of plotting and working methods of Nathan were outside her realm of comprehension. Quite in line with feminine tendency, Caroline believed in her intuitive intelligence to thwart Nathan's plot with a series of her own counter plans and actions. She had no such political acumen and exposure as to match wily Nathan's political games.

In one such regular inflow of feedback, Caroline got to know the tip of the iceberg on the treacherous plot devised by Nathan and his troublous goons to sabotage the welfare and public awareness programs that CWPN conducted in the constituency. Traversing the tip further, Caroline wholly unraveled Nathan's sinuous plot, described by a code name 'strike the hot iron', of engaging a killer team of wholly adolescent and well-trained kids, like in a Hollywood thriller, to liquidate Brian or invalidate him physically in one of his social rounds of meetings with his general public.

All unimaginable but swift twists, shockers, and games are politics' own privy fiefdom. Theatrical and movie production units, without any copyright and legal compensation, spread the ploy as entertainment, adopted in social and cultural gatherings, and educational programs. This idea is a twister, as politics is the sole creative origin, shock, and stumbler in all parts of the world.

Unable to contain and counter Nathan's wits and cunning moves anymore, Caroline met Brian on one of his relaxed evenings and updated him with all the intricate details of Nathan's plot. It was not a shocker for Brian; he knew Nathan as a slithering snake.

What amazed Brian was the level of Caroline's grasping of the situation and her ability to swing into action. He was in awe of her;. This girl has an owl's eyes to track nocturnal activities too, and she has a spontaneous ability to tackle problems.. *'She needs just a little bit of molding. What she needs is fine attuning of her time sense, course of action, and merciless attitude for execution, and she will be ready to assume her political office any moment,'* he was loud to himself. Yet, outwardly, he responded to her, "I am well aware of the grave situation, and I will be on guard to some extent." 'To some extent', he reflected the restricted human tendency.

"I appreciate your genuine concern for my security. You can reach me directly at any time and continue with your good work, keep me updated on the latest developments both in our party and in our opponents' camps, and act suitably with my consent," Brian concluded his meeting with her.

Caroline summoned a few of her trusted and talented marshals and deployed them inside

Nathan's ranks. The marshals were closely knit in various essential workforces like bartenders, security personnel, and chauffeurs to provide services to top party leaders and office bearers. They were military-trained and assigned to espionage on Nathan's political activities and sources of various financial and organizational support for his political outfit.

Caroline was now sure of her plan to disintegrate Nathan's organizational support. The leaders from each field with loyal party troops were invited to the party's headquarters and held group parleys and individual discussions with disgruntled opportunists for their support to Brian's CWPN. In her next move of tactical maneuver to Nathan's game, she suggested Brian dismiss George from the party's primary membership and send him back to Nathan on a specific feeler mission for easy access to the opposition's top-level members.

NOMINATION FOR ELECTION

Trying to locate his SSN card to fill in the nomination form for the forthcoming election, Brian raked up repeatedly the entire tall wooden storage cabinet and was irked with himself for not remembering to retrieve it from its location. Brian called, "Ramona, can you please come here and help me get my SSN card?"

Ramona, quite busy in her morning schedule with making breakfast and coffee, besides getting their children, Natasha and Ambrose, ready for school, was inattentive to his call.

"You are not listening to me at all. I called you twice, and I'm pressed for time. Come and help me get my SSN card," Brian urged Ramona. Then, realizing that something was important, she rushed to Brian, and after listening to him on his morning episode, she said, "Brian, the school bus is now due to arrive at any moment. Let us see our children off to board their school bus. I will try to get it immediately in a second thereafter. Please stay calm," Ramona was just practical.

Ramona then busied herself to locate the SSN card and searched all over again in the cabinet, TV shelf, and book stands. "Here, I got it for you, Brian," she was really jubilant, not because she had succeeded in the much time-pressed job, but because she was able to help Brian with his schedule. Brian somewhat felt guilty for entertaining undue grouse against her and in a way of saying 'Thank you, Ramona,' kissed her on the cheeks, then picked up his lunch bag along with all important files and bid adieu to pursue his objective.

After their playtime in the evening, Ramona urged both children to complete their homework and oversaw their studious involvement in it. The children then pestered her to watch their favorite soccer games on TV, and she readily complied with their demands. As night crept in, the children went to sleep with a 'good night' kiss to their mom. Ramona, gazing at the clock ticking half-past ten, realized that Brian had not yet returned home. 'Probably too much workload,' she consoled herself while looking for his car in the portico.

Parking his car in the hangar, Brian briskly paced his steps carrying an empty lunch bag and large files in his left hand, and a small 'Cash & Carry' paper bag swinging in his right hand. Ramona also noticed his pervasive joy and pretended to be casual. Tossing his left-hand baggage and placing the right-hand carry bag softly on the dining table, Brian hugged Ramona and lifted her loftily in a whirling motion, planting a soft kiss on her forehead and on her cheeks. Ramona knew by now all about Brian and guessed correctly that this was his way of making up for the mood of his morning rupture.

ELECTION CAMPAIGN

The general election schedule was fixed, and the disputed symbols of warring parties were frozen. The trend and multiplication of new parties that jumped into the election foray amazed the general electorate. "Were the candidates that eager to push themselves into public service?" and "Until the last election, they were untraceable, so why now and from where did so many contestants appear?" were some of the obvious questions the electorate wanted to ask but did not.

All election wards were buzzing with volunteers, fans, party workers, and curious onlookers. The party workers' houses were partly converted to temporary warehouses for the storage of propaganda materials. The list of propaganda materials stretched from colorful profiles of the contesting candidates to paper inserts and notices, danglers and banners, electronic signboards, musical instruments and amplifiers, printed t-shirts with the party's logo, and two-wheelers and mini carrier vans parked outside their houses on the roads.

Ramona, as one of the ordinary members, took part in the party's election meetings held at the headquarters with Brian, Caroline, and regional leaders. "Failure always hugs you when you are unaware of what you are doing," Ramona began her reassuring introduction, "and it's a gateway to proceed, not a destination of your journey."

"We commence our campaign with systematic planning and disciplined 'step by step' execution without any further delay. Stay united and go beyond all barriers to your success. I now end this beginner with the hope of seeing you with your 'big smile' post the election results. Good Luck," Ramona moved aside.

Caroline, as the Public Relations Manager, spoke briefly about the method of campaigning in four precise steps:

- Not more than 2-3 volunteers would visit each household and meet the senior women residents to explain their purpose of the visit to update on our party represented by the candidate.

  One copy of our printed pamphlet will be handed over to her. They would request her to vote for our party for her own progress and welfare.

- Another batch of 2-3 party workers, visiting the household, would verify the eligible voters while handing over the official printed voter identity cards. They would politely remind them to vote for our party and offer their help or service without any commitment.

The volunteers, who for the first time visited, accompanied by a senior lady representative from our party would call on the senior women resident and after exchanging little pleasantries, would make an appeal personally to her to vote along with her family members to our party's representative solely for her welfare.

- Just two days prior to polling, the candidate, along with earlier visits to party workers, with a pleasant disposition, would collectively and individually appeal to all the voters while facing the senior women in households.

A brief audio presentation of these model guidelines was displayed on the silver screen to the audience in the hall. Caroline invited the members present to seek clarification if they ever so desired.

Directly looking at Ramona and Brian, she spoke, "Our party workers and volunteers would, wearing the party's clean and neat uniform dress, carry placards displaying the party logo, manifesto, and the candidate's photo. There is no relaxation to this code."

While concluding her brief outline on the campaign model, Caroline decisively made her point transparent that at no point in time or place would our volunteers and party workers adopt aggressive outbursts or react and retort even at the slightest provocation.

NATHAN'S GAME OF POLITICS

Nathan's national level of influence and hold in the lower ranks of the party were dwindling. Enraged with the deprivation of all hitherto ego-boosting power and attention, Nathan fell victim to his own game, and his vengeance goaded him to devise a venomous plan that would sabotage Brian in his public career. Sensing the tussle within the top brass, the office bearers and party workers became rude and behaved antagonistically toward the public. Their selfishness for personal pecuniary gains grew like an ogre.

Amidst all this melee, George shifted his loyalty to save his skin, so George deserting Nathan in his very critical and solitary situation was like 'adding fuel to the fire'. Nathan bated out of breath, swore to teach a fitting lesson to all these 'chameleons'.

Our inherent ability to foresee that all evil designs and actions have a more significant impact on us than on our rivals is dormant, and we realize that with our advancing age and enriching experience!

Assembling all hostile political members, Nathan chalked out a tentative program. With his penetrating unsocial elements, he saw to it that some of his left-wing henchmen were deployed in select jobs at the base camp of Brian. They were all assigned with the specific and heinous task of region-wise network espionage on activities carried out by Brian and his party members. This network exposed the opponents' original plan, and Nathan and his gang knew the plan and the corresponding action more accurately than the actual members of Brian's party.

George returned to Nathan with swollen eyes and a sunken face, all showing his inexplicable suffering. Added to this was Brian's indifferent attitude and behavioral neglect towards him. All ears to George, Nathan shook his head for a moment, in total disbelief that one of his able lieutenants, George, had undergone such humiliation and ignominy. Of course, he was sadistically happy about whatever had happened to George in his opponent's camp, but at the same time, his mind cautioned him to consider that this was probably Brian's tactical play against him. Pretending to fall for George's theatrics and continuing his disbelief toward George for all his earlier foul moves, Nathan aimed to checkmate Brian in his own game. He scheduled a series of public events, with a direct call to all people in his campaign. On all fronts, George was pitted.

STRATEGIC CAMPAIGN & ELECTION VIOLENCE

The tempo was building up with every feverish moment. The national media, frenziedly buzzing about their blitzkrieg on Nathan and Brian, their focus on the whole nation, and their competitive rivalry on their political fronts, created a clear and wide coverage to edge their competition in the national media. Their social policies, programs, and welfare schemes were probed, analyzed, supported by the pro-parties, and attacked vehemently by their opposition.

In a piquant crowded election rally charged with an electric atmosphere, Brian gathered all of his volunteers and posed a puzzle, "Who, in your old age and solitude, would you visualize as two of the most important persons in your life? And why?" All answers 'Mother', 'My sister', 'my class teacher', 'wife', and 'daughter' from the participants flowed coherently, with a convenient omission of 'why'.

Brian observed that these responses collectively and quite figuratively pointed to only women and, alas, there was no trace of ever a man featured in the survey to show as a 'sample' of masculine gender!

This gave a clue and an unflinching belief to form a strong base for his campaign with the majority of women volunteers and to concentrate all his efforts to reach out to eligible women electorate and then, through them, the other general voters.

The party workers also canvassed on every platform and beat so methodically assigned, and the feverish pitch did not seem to abate while the noisy movement of the general public stamped a sense of approval for the contestants' courteous visits to the electorate.

"This momentum is slated to culminate in a climax on the polling day, the 15th of December, and with results announcing the electoral winners after 3 days, all this public campaign machinery will rest for the next four years, and you may not get another chance. But *now this is our moment and we all need to support our nation in its attempt to leap forward* economically and in all its scientific experiments." appealed Brian to his people in his concluding campaign.

This was undoubtedly electric and absolutely a winning strategy!

With its euphoria always reserved for the ruling party, the media was awestruck by Brian's genuine intent and adopted its favorable disposition on all visual platforms. Such was the level of hysteria streaming in the mornings, evenings, bus stands, railway stations, public and government offices, and everywhere.

All the big and small population clusters - be they well-developed or underdeveloped villages, towns, and cities were under the grip of these volunteers who, with the party's logo bands worn on top of their left arm, moved very punctiliously in groups to distribute leaflets and pamphlets of their party's manifesto and the polling contestants' details within the constituency.

Brian's army of volunteers took on the onerous task of educating the public on their policies in public forums, digital platforms, and, above all, the important one-to-one visits to the electorate. Now, aware of the welfare policies, the electorate has gained additional impetus!

Something was amiss! Nathan was a crafty 'center-forward player', who always kept all his political stalwarts and the media at his tender hooks. The media was silent as his national activities never saw daylight.

This greatly bothered Brian.

George from Nathan's tent was in full tornado mode campaign, strategically finalizing the party's poll manifesto, deploying an army of party workers and electronic musical instruments to play the voters' choicest film music with folklore dancing to their tunes and steps and chorus appeal for support to their party nominees. Adopting military discipline, he oversaw his contesting candidate's profile, displaying posters, danglers, and the party's flags fluttering in all the corners.

In a countermove to check Brian's growing popularity, George, with all of his local chieftains, was meeting the candidates all on a personal plane and tirelessly cajoled them to visit and meet the voters of their constituency. Their meetings with the people were scheduled rotationally to avoid direct encounters with opposition camps. This tactic was more of a morale fillip to the contestants and party workers and brightened the overall prospects of his party NDWF as well.

It was a military dedication, and the people who saw military parades only on TV shows were overwhelmed by their 'meticulous working attitude'. Some good lessons from such political maneuvers, too, we got to learn, but we detested perhaps because of our prejudice. At the same time, while enjoying the intra-party rivals, we endorsed our tacit approval and encouraged their sabotage to spoil the party's performance in the electorate. We were then penalized to accept the debacle meted out by the people's verdict because we failed to grasp those hints, earlier deemed as insignificant, from the opposition camps and dump them ignominiously.

In some pro-party pockets, the party men from both sides vied for strong canvassing of electorate support. The electorate decorum was, to a large extent, reduced as they aggressively led the voters to swear, or else enslaved them with gifts and favors.

The stiff competitive insurgence of the opposition, the volunteers' outbursts, and their repeated unruly behavior caused chaos and psychological fear in the minds of the general public regarding their safety. Some sporadic violence inevitably occurred, which impacted public utilities and institutional properties. Of course, both rival parties moved fervently with their objective singularly focused on winning the electorate, and it was their main aim to avert and dodge all untoward happenings due to the proximate campaign closure and polling schedules.

The police, overburdened with their existing tasks, were left with no alternative but to resort to tear gas shelling, wielding batons, and all that within their operational norms to enforce the dispersal of violent mobs. The political goons engaged in arson and violence for the expansion of their political mileage.

As is the case with every normal society, the public always bears the ultimate brunt of the responsibility for colossal damages to property, transport, market wares, personal injury, and casualties. The mischief-mongers have escaped from the clutches of the law until now.

This, of course, was the bane for Nathan, and his rejection from the electorate fueled his hell-bent revenge for his party's total rout from political power.

PEOPLES' VERDICT

Terror, money, and political goons considerably enjoyed society's disinclined but fear-based vocal support. Every nation witnessed the under-reports on such horrendous loss of lives and sufferings of the general populace, besides the inflicted damage on the infrastructural network, to control the erosion of public faith in the administrative machinery.

Charged with hatred and wrath over Nathan's villainous acts just before the election and with only one way open, and rather forced, to choose Brian's party for their welfare, the national electorate voted for Brian's CWPN - Common Welfare and Progress of our Nation - to power, albeit with a wafer-thin majority!

The victory parade with drum beats in tune with local musical groups, bunches of balloons floating in the air all over the venue, party cadres and the public high on physical spirits without liquid spirits dancing to their music, Hallelujah, such a gaiety of abandon mood ought not to be missed out!

NATHAN'S REVENGE

The maestro of wicked politics, Nathan, was tipped well beforehand about Brian's public schedules in a series of open and thanksgiving symposia on Hitchcock Avenue and Roosevelt Square on the ensuing Saturday and Sunday. "This is a golden opportunity for me to remove my political enemy, Brian," Nathan avowed himself to scheme a series of successive actions.

Surveying the whole area from which to choose one spot that would afford a secluded and undetectable but very clear view of the auditorium, Nathan meticulously charted his method of operation.

In his initial move and without disclosing his identity, he engaged two of his ace shooters into his confidence and took repeated trials of their marksmanship, obviously to draw a hint of sadistic confidence.

With all available details of schedules and statistics, Nathan and his team worked on likely wind speed, the long range of the semi-automatic rifles in use, the camera angle, and the time slot in the total scheme of the first political killing.

From the gate of the central hall, he tested with particular clarity if he could spot the operation site and if so, how much time the private detectives and police personnel would take to locate and how fast they would reach the site. Still unsatisfied, he was going through the operational details very carefully.

Nathan, watching all political activities from the center podium, swiftly brought his ace team to the 19th-floor apartment of the forty-story building 'Windsor Manor' and surveyed every place to pinpoint the target spot. He chose the 19th floor mainly to provide his team with a safe escape route via the fire lift from the spot in the event of any mishap and, at the same time, to deceive the police and delay their arrival at the crime scene.

Nathan was going around the building and he came across an ice storage warehouse at the floor level of the adjacent building 'Lands View'. Taking a penetrative survey of the building, he worked out a method to reduce the escape time from the 19th floor of Windsor Manor through the floor level of Lands View. He then explained the details of the escape route from the 19th floor to the adjacent Lands View, then to flee in the parked car outside, and the time slot to shoot just seconds after the swearing-in of Brian.

Nathan marked the position of his two ace shooters, one from the 19th-floor right wing aiming at the swearing-in podium and the other standing at the left-wing one floor below aiming at his target. The way he planned very minutely, he was a master strategist par excellence; alas, he willfully diverted to engage himself in wicked ways.

BRIAN'S PERSONAL LOSS

The jubilant CWPN party members assembled in the august auditorium of the Secretariat in the capital, some to participate in the swearing-in ceremony, the majority to witness and endorse their wholehearted support for the ruling party.

The Governor General, draped in his official attire, exuded his authoritative dignity as he entered the assembly chambers with his forward and backward personal security cadets' cover. Glancing at the assembly per his eagle eyes, he surmised that the chamber was in impeccable order for the conduct of its business. Brian and Ramona were seated in the front row. Caroline, the Public Relations Manager, surrounded by friends, well-wishers, a few dependable party allies, and marshals, was seated a row behind.

The Governor General then invited Mr Brian to the podium. With his imperious nod on the arrangements made, the President signaled the Chief Justice to administer the ceremonial swearing-in of the new senate body.

Ramona, with her feminine intuition, was uneasy and looked around to see if anything was quite unusual. Yet, unable to comprehend and to ease herself from her sitting posture to some extent, she got up from her seat, quite indiscreet and out of her etiquette befitting the ceremony. What then prompted her, she alone knew, to look at the right wing of the adjacent building. Abruptly pushed by her own self to lean in front of Brian and, with both hands spread wide, brushed him and others aside out of danger. Then, only a 'thud' arose instantly. Ramona lay on the ground with blood oozing from her body.

A few seconds earlier, enthusiasm, gaiety, and hope overflowed! The viewers and invitees, realizing the horror that struck during the ceremony, were frozen.

Caroline, until now seated in the second row of the podium, saw what was happening and sprinted at lightning speed to reach the commotion site. While clearing the crowd swiftly, she called an ambulance and emergency medical help, police, and military back-up to quell the unrest.

Pandemonium erupted in the assembly chambers as an ambulance, brushing the viewers aside, was shifting the breathless Ramona to the ambulance, hurriedly speeding to the state-owned hospital. The experienced and professional medical team, accompanied by the technical support team and hospital service providers including the blood bank, were well on the spot, administering the revival operations. Then, suddenly, the cardiograph beeped a straight red line, despite their nonstop efforts. The medical team tragically hung its head, and the effervescent Ramona vaporized with her last breath from her real human self!

RAMONA'S FINAL JOURNEY

For the first time, Destiny and the Lord of Death, Azrael, till now called cruel, merciless, and other despicable nicknames, looked derisively at the Lord of Creations as well as at the Lord of the Eternal Savior, and asked them, "What do you think of my job? Isn't this now the best of all my feats?" The gods, yet to comprehend, stared blankly at Azrael, unable to read his mischief, and then looked down at the earthen soil.

There, Ramona, one of the most affable women on earth, was laid in a new and open glass coffin, with round and decorative wreaths embellished all over and the final sermon underway, all well set up for her final voyage.

The flower vendor ruefully observed, "Very few flowers and attendees for good functions and unlimited for the departed."

Brian, his great-grandsons being the pallbearers flanked by granddaughters and a score of their close relatives and friends, were slowly inching under thin drizzles. The party members and neighbors all mourning in procession, eminent and rich personalities from various societies flanked by social outcasts aside, were following them to pay obeisance, with umbrellas open.

Ramona brought all people together, pounding her staunch faith that only the human life that cares for fellow human feelings rises above all difficult fences. Some people who were star beneficiaries of her help beyond time and distance were crestfallen.

Now the Lord of Death, Azrael, explained, "When you were alive but failed to show compassion and care for your fellows and did nothing within your capacity to lessen their misery, you were dead. *Compassion and love to assuage fellow human beings' misery made the person live forever in their minds, even after death.*" That was what we considered as 'life enriched' with a sole purpose.

"Your best child, Ramona, did what she could seriously while she was alive, and the angels here wanted her so lovingly with them." The Lords of Creation and Savior were dim-witted to retort or agitate.

Besides them, the other angels were silently present with their lightning, thunder, rainstorms, and gales, participating in her final journey to lay the cabin in the marshy soil, a little away from all other mortals.

The intimidating and inundated rival tendencies of all the natural greenery, bluish expanse, waters, and brown mountains, the wild and soft creatures were still, all mourning in silence, just as a solid testament to Ramona's affable personality.

The media was seized with total shock at the unexpected happenings and quickly moved to flash the sad news in its national coverage. The various celebrity-owned TV channels, government-run radio stations, and public platforms all blared raucously about this tragic event with repeated exposures untiringly.

When the gods looked again at Asrael, he quizzed the gods, "Are you both now up for something of a new world? Oh, is that why you both engaged me with this task?" He bid adieu ruefully to continue with his work. Ruefully, yes, because he, too, experienced human feelings of anguish with Ramona's death!

Women in all of their seasons like grandmother, mother, sister, wife, daughter, granddaughter, and other forms silently sacrifice themselves to prop up their best man's 'always bruised' ego and extend their generation.

BRIAN'S LUNATIC SWINGS

Brian was still not able to recover his normal self, feeling isolated with his young children. All too sudden tragic happenings suspended his clarity of direction, his mind wavering from one end of despair to the other extreme end of inconclusive lamentation.

Carolina, for her part, used her warm companionship to infuse a little more moral spirit in Brian and bring him back to his active schedule but saw all of her efforts melting. If anything, her constant solace propped him up from his inert existence.

With Brian's guidance in her early days in public service, she was making decisions on the party's affairs and administrative matters to ensure the smooth flow of its public policy through the party ranks and media. She selected Palmer, Smita, and Vedika, three of her most dependable friends from her school days, and deployed them in crucial functions. Through them, she periodically guided the governmental functionaries on important policies and projects. At the same time, she restricted herself to the higher levels of operation so as not to impose herself or be construed as interfering in their functions. In this way, she was able to streamline the disciplined involvement of the workforce while maintaining her personal influence to oversee government and party functions.

With her daily activity in the care of Brian and his children on the one hand, and on the other, inducting Brian gradually into important public affairs, Carolina acted decisively to eliminate the loss of time and to officially adopt her decisions and confirm her initial actions. This, though a very agonizing operation for her, helped Brian return to his normal senses.

POLICE ACTION

With swift alertness, the police and security guards sped to the spot and cordoned off the whole area, cautiously monitoring to nab the culprits who had taken shelter in the hideous electrical room on the mezzanine floor between the lift and stairway, which is normally overlooked by passers-by and residents.

After carefully combing the buildings, the police captured both felony contractors, mercilessly handcuffing each other and swiftly moving them in a heavily guarded police van. Quite ironically, the culprits were given heavy security!

During the grilling interrogations and tactical cross-examinations of the culprits, the duo gave a sketchy picture that resembled the man incognito and who contracted them for a hefty compensation. The police force, matching numerous records and photographs of a number of criminals, came to properly identify the mastermind as 'Nathan' and circulated his sketch under 'wanted' posters. The land and air passageways were sealed, and an alert notice on the criminal 'show' was publicly displayed to nab him.

Nathan's classic methodology and years of his public life melted into public oblivion, and he was still running elusively from the law's punitive grip!

(3) PRIZE: BRIAN'S ASCENDANCY

When we are sure of something, life reverses our tendency. Brian again remembered this lesson while trying to keep his emotions and his trembling body in check. His mind was roving mentally about intimate moments of his companionship with Ramona over two decades since their wedlock and it flipped through a few freak anger and misunderstanding scenes, all in its own lopsided references. Her demise benumbed his sense of reality. In his effort to console Brian, the Governor-General rescheduled his swearing-in for the following Wednesday evening at 05.00 p.m.

Brian was still not able to recover his normal schedule, feeling depressed and isolated together with his young children.

The revised schedule of swearing-in was slated to afford Brian to overcome his tragic loss. But this purpose went astray as Brian nearly stumbled with his cognitive faculties. This situation warranted the stationing of the emergency medical team beside his bed in his chambers to monitor in close observation. They administered periodic doses of sedatives to help soothe him in his mental turmoil to recuperate his health.

Fortune smiled at its favorite child! Brian woke up, looked around to see the medical attendants, and stared at the wall calendar displaying Wednesday, 9th March 2014. He spontaneously remembered that his swearing-in was scheduled for today.

On his confusion about what happened in the interim period, he demanded information from the medical team, who were very courteous to update him on his temporary hibernation and the prescribed medical treatment in the last two days. There was not much time left for the ceremony, and he felt pain in his temples and forehead. Swallowing a painkiller instantly, he rushed himself to get ready while calling his party members on their action schedule. They were directed to update the program to other members of the party. He made it clear that all his lieutenants should be at the august hall by 4.30 p.m.and directed them to enforce discipline and ensure decorum in the audience.

In the cluster of all emotional run-down, Brian felt propelled towards his work schedule and swore to assume the highest office of the nation. The Lord said, "When one door is closed for you, I keep the other open for you!"

The customary congratulations and celebratory procession all took a backseat, the gloomy situation still weighing on the minds of the people.

He implored all the elected members of his party, "There are times that will bury you all in your personal sentiments and spirits, just like my experience now. At the same time, your duties cannot wait until you overcome your personal feelings. There is always a sunrise. Your time is now calling you towards your duty. So, the best way is to keep all the diversions, troubles, and pressures at bay. Dedicate unflinchingly and work untiringly for the nation's welfare."

Consequently, upon his opening address, Brian inducted his able and dependable coterie into his cabinet, with important portfolios disbursed. In a very private in-camera meeting, Brian reiterated to his ministers the chaotic state of affairs, the urgency of law and order, coupled with the drastically needed economic thrust and eroding people's faith.

At the dimly lit left corner of the ceremonial auditorium stood a woman in her late forties, pleasingly clad and with an angelic profile. Looking sideways, forward, and backward, she was nervous and looked around to see if anybody would recognize her. Thank Heavens, people's oblivion is a boon for her!

Brian walked to the podium and exchanged greetings with the Governor General, who signaled the Justice to initiate the ceremony. Alongside the officiating Justice, Brian was conscious of his swearing-in, and he stood still before the mic, looking at the audience, row after row. Gaiety and cheerful moods pervaded, and a thunderous ovation rose, with people shaking hands and exchanging pleasantries among themselves. Brian, following his protocol, moved from one dignitary to another. Bouquets and compliments piled up, and there, when he saw an old woman farthest in the left corner of the assembly, his gaze abruptly, without any reason, fixed on her.

She was familiar and yet, he was unable to identify her correctly. He paused his inaugural speech and was thinking whether there would be any connection between her and him. His mind grew curious!

With one of his officers assigned for chaperoning her to the podium, Brian was elated to identify her, hugged her, and exclaimed, "Madam Ariane, it was a pleasant surprise for me to see you here. Why were you standing as a common citizen at the farthest back there? You have a seat next to me and be relaxed."

Then, he turned to the audience and narrated how Madam Ariane molded his early childhood days, imbuing faith and principles to reach the goal. "My dear fellow citizens, if for whatever reason I am standing here before you, it is definitely all because of her unselfish care and attention to me for so many years and without any expectation of return. Dear August guests and party members, we need more people like Madam Ariane to create young leaders for our nation to lead other countries. Please give a big ovation to my mentor, Madam Ariane." Thunderous applause blushed the high skies, spreading its pink cheeks across the entire western horizon. The ovation subsided slowly for a long time thereafter.

Ariane, for her part, gave him a big and his most cherished souvenir *"By misdeeds, you can cheat your PRESENT! Not your FUTURE!!"* and lovingly hugged him.

"Dear Son, you have chosen the right path and I am glad about that. Sometimes you may be all alone. More often than not, you will face yourself with an impasse or predicament to question yourself, *What if I don't want to do what I am doing now?* Be clear and firm in your vision and pursue reaching where you need to."

Brian gently took the souvenir, fondly looked at the front and back, and flipped through like a child! His mentor, Ariane, took note of his action, her heart filled with immense joy.

"Come to me whenever you want some space and engage in some silly talks with me. I will make your favorite steak, egg pudding, and frothing coffee."

She was about to take leave and then turned abruptly to speak, "Son, I need just one and only one favor from you. You just said, 'this country has to lead other nations, right?' So, among your hard-pressed work schedules, give some time to locate, identify, and foster new generation leaders to follow you and fulfill your goals."

Oh my God, this sixty-plus lady was a real stateswoman!

For a very long time, he was staring at his mentor and he experienced an obscure emotional drain of his soul parting; his tears popped up through his cheeks to bid adieu as Ariane took leave from him!

Brushing this downcast sentiment aside, he walked heavily into his Secretariat and saw members on one side and files piled on the other. 'I've got to stay focused on my passion,' he asked himself, 'and what is my passion?'

Brian classified priority actions for his people's prosperity and their security. Leafing from the disorder as a result of his wife Ramona's sacrificial death in the Secretariat, he deployed a massive police force armed with power and transport mobility to ruthlessly quell all the anti-social activities. In addition, he introduced different productivity-based commercial movements of labor and material without loss of time and damage. The efficiency of his administration in the background of delegation of the responsible area of operation revived his subjects' morality and boosted the inflow of funds which, in turn, soothed the rioting public partly. It was now an opportune time for steps to improve the social texture on education, finance, health, and infrastructural boosts. The local administration was empowered to increase the mandatory free schooling up to the undergraduate level, to license the experienced merchant houses for the fair conduct of all financial transactions, to the medical fraternity for the smooth conduct of health and hospital services, besides scores of other paramount facilities including curtailing and discouraging the disruptive antisocial elements while meting out the legal sentence to the criminals so adjudged.

He is often astonished to realize *how apt the simile is between mind and ocean, both are calm, sometimes ferociously turbulent, and have no shores!*

No human being ever claimed or succeeded to fathom their depth and flow.

Coming back from his disoriented moments, he summoned Caroline and allocated the portfolios for both improving and strengthening the party's regional units. With this, he suggested revamping the organizational structure, inducting new members, and involving them in local cultural festivals to promote the party's reputation.

Caroline, in her fervor to join the ministerial berth, hid her disappointment, and Brian did not fail to take note of that. He abruptly remembered how his erstwhile colleague Cynthia deserted him at the most inopportune moment and did not want any such setback in his current functions. Probably, he believed firmly in Caroline's intellect and composure. Besides, the reason why he desisted from his impulse to induct her into the cabinet was his prerogative in the interests of the efficient functioning of the administration.

COURT SCENES

The court where the captive Mr Nathan with his confederates standing in the box was cordoned off from the news channels, the political influence, and the general public. The court, however, set in-camera proceedings for a later-day public broadcast.

Contrary to the conclusive evidence presented in the court of law, Mr Nathan vehemently denied his involvement in the shoot-out and the instant killing of Ramona in the Assembly Hall. He maintained his sanctimonious posture, cohesively asserting that his political opponents had vengeful roles as an orchestrated team to entrap him in this heinous plot and blemish his political life.

It was an easy task for the Police, Crime Investigative, and Law Enforcement teams to nab the accused, and yet the sequential arguments and statements of both public and defense counsels, the chaotic court scenes on cognizance of the crime, the verdict on the accused as the culprit to mete punitive sentence dragged the time-wheel slowly.

The public counsel intensely pictured the crime scene in sequences of one incident after another, all of which then translated as a gruesome motive for the murder of a hapless spectator. The public counsel's eloquent arguments and presentations were irrefutably logical, and his recreation transported the court to the actual happening of the crime. The court and the public witnessing the scene felt as though the public counsel was an onlooker at the time of the incident.

The defense counsel drew public antipathy and jeered at him as he attempted with all his wits to extenuate the serious nature of the crime, suggesting that the hoisted attempt was just an action inefficiently drafted by some other political agents to assassinate the politically elected and acclaimed representative.

The defense, in his veiled bid to prove, submitted that his client was unduly charged with the commitment of palpable homicide. He, in the end, played to Nathan's opening tune that "his political rivals had stained their hands thus to entrap him" and to be absolved of his crime in consideration of his public contributions.

"Any influential or political force that curbs the social texture as a deviation and bends it unethically in its evil design for personal gain does not escape from the law of the land. Our law should not provide umbrella protection to perpetrators of social villains for circumventing the law, which will send the wrong message to the public at large."

"May the bench with its par-excellence wisdom reckon the case on the wicked motive of the killing of a common spectator. Our Guardians of Justice need to bring their minds back to the basic tenet of law that the common man has every right to pursue his choice of occupation conforming to social standards and anywhere within the region's political and legal frame."

Thus, the public counsel conclusively established Nathan's motive to spoil Brian's public and family life.

The public counsel concluded his arguments, and when he thanked the court for its forbearance, the bench of the jury headed by the Judge awoke from its slumber by shaking their heads furiously. Was it in disapproval of the arguments? Or would that mean they all thanked him for his conclusive submission? In one angle, they all looked uninvolved, obviously.

The crowd, led by the bar benches, joined in the thunderous ovation with a rather quizzical expectation of the final verdict.

BRIAN'S RETURN

Without awaiting the judgment, Brian left the court for his political chambers to proceed with his assignments that had long been pending his attention for sanction, disposal, and reconsideration. As he delved deeply into the current status of various welfare projects, he noticed that most of the projects had exceeded their time and cost estimates solely due to his melancholy, which brought a sharp realization that all sad and happy events had a temporary emotional impact on the daily lives of universal subjects. Their welfare remained constant as long as life extended, and his purpose to contribute was steadfast.

With his existing mental makeup, Brian contemplated establishing continuity of various welfare projects with modifications to suit the changing demands of the time. He called Carolina and her political and party aides to a conference to exchange his views and find a way out of this peculiar scene.

The confidant lieutenants assembled, rather perplexed, and their minds, which till now lay inebriated, worked in full efficiency for the abrupt meeting.

"We borrow our body and mind from our mothers, to be nurtured and cultured by other women who come as spouses and daughters in our later-year lives. My experience with my wife Ramona's death, by any means, is still an emotional vacuum. But that does not allow me to dwell constantly in depression and sadness, so much as to neglect my national duties to the living people's welfare. The national duties, which involve peaceful living with our brethren, we all assumed willingly on our shoulders."

"You are here assembled to find a stable way to develop and ensure continuity and execution of our current projects that would, in the long run, provide some succor for their current incommodious moments. The solution you all attempt to work out needs to be insulated against compromising or diluting methods to meet greedy interests."

"We now take our tea recess over which some of you may be inclined to superficially discuss with your other mates to get the feel of this matter." Thus, Brian suspended the assembly and returned to his chambers for a brief personal space.

Over the tea break, the members were engaged in an intense discussion on the arrangement of their boss and transitioned to other topics. Caroline, with her stern reminder, disciplined them to stick to their tasks, "If we could not work out an agreeable solution, we would better stay together on the job." That brought their focus back.

On resumption, Brian invited the members to present their ideas and solutions, to which their response was mere silence. Their hesitation brought Brian forth to the meeting to explain his motto, "The prime physical efficiency does not grow in tandem with the growing years of mental maturity. In our old age, we need more shelter and health facilities to be pampered with a little love from our own people, friends, and relatives included. Our projects, stalled with a lack of our commitment, would speed us to our eternal sleep out of our suffering and not by Nature. "Do you all understand me? How birth and death continue despite an all-natural holocaust, our welfare project, too, needs to continue for all those distressed. How do we sustain their continuity?" he surveyed around and explained, "Every project would extend a minimum period of 3-5 years for its completion and efficient functioning thereafter. Our physical ability diminishes with the passage of time in the process. This necessitates fresh and unbridled talents to pour in. Dedicated in the initial years of the projects, these unbridled talents contribute enormously to steady and boost the welfare of their kinsmen."

"We now need to devise a political system to bring in new commandants and train them in their chosen area of function to the utmost efficiency. These commandants would work in their initial phase under the supervision of their bosses until they assume total accountability for a brief tenure or until the next usurper assumes."

"With this stream of thoughts coupled with the short term of a person's active personal or public life running in my mind, I consider it very important for me to induct new people gifted with focus and talents in the national arena."

"You all have administrative roles involving various tasks and an unfriendly atmosphere. What is imperative to sustain in such a hostile environment is a person's direct involvement with the public to garner their unflinching support."

"Caroline rose and assumed the responsibility of discharging all my functional duties to the best of her logic, interweaving personal rhythm, during my convalescence from depression. Besides, she was well-trained in our party's functions and public life under the aegis of my wife, Ramona. The three of you have all stayed together and shouldered the responsibility to perform well."

"From my observation, without any personal bias, Caroline would qualify well in the president's chambers, allowing me to retire from public life. With her political acumen and public welfare policy background, she will steer the National finance, defense, and social agenda. To achieve this goal, it is imperative that the four of you stay glued to one another in your functions and communications."

"Of course, you all have your right to act as you deem fit and ample discretion at your disposal. We will be taking a vote among the four of you, by secret ballot, in the next one hour, and each of you will have just one vote."

LOYALTY
LIVE ON YOUR AMBITION
LIMITED TO YOURSELF!

The three lieutenants Palmer, Smita, and Vedika sat around Caroline, and at the initial stage of the exchanges of opinion and views on policies and plans, the quad were amiable, accepting and approving some points and vociferously discounting other 'not-so-important' public affair policies. It was then transparent that they would arrive at a cordial choice of their leader.

Lo, it was just a mirage, and politics had no lineage!

The next two hours passed, each expressing capabilities of her own, and, in the background of her experience and understanding of national politics, each pined to be at the helm. Emotions and selfish interests erupted sky-high, and the noise levels peaked at their decibels.

With no solution in close view, Caroline offered to step aside and work with any one of the other three, one of whom they all conscientiously elected to lead them as a team. Caroline, at the same time, realized a wee bit of pain and disappointment that her own friends didn't come to place her unanimously at the National capital. Her outlook on integrity, her own dreams to contribute to public welfare growth, and to some extent, her personality of governance faded to a thin layer on the horizon!

Sensing her aloofness and despair and giving momentary thought to her voluntary contributions to the general public, Brian decided on his choice: "I will be endorsing my vote to Caroline."

Prefer to choose only two among all the four candidates to make the selection possible, Palmer and Smita sullenly withdrew from the arena, and there remained only Caroline and Vedika.

Caroline emerged as the winner of the nation's prestigious office, and Vedika was also sworn in along with Palmer and Smita.

The national politics took a toll on Brian, who now felt drained of his energy and enthusiasm and bid farewell to the new incumbents.

It was a mix of calm composure in the dawn and a twilight experience of relinquishing his own self from the active public role to one of the passive spectators in the mainstream. Brian was unable to grow up!

EPILOGUE

We begin our lives with open minds, nurtured by our mothers who selflessly prioritize our needs over their own, enduring physical hardships and mental anxieties.

In this environment of unconditional love, we are instilled with culture, discipline, and dedication. As we grow, teachers enter our lives, dedicating their time and immense patience to our academic, physical, and athletic development.

With such a solid foundation laid in our early years to withstand future challenges, our first act of repayment often becomes the convenient forgetting of their contributions to our growth.

The essence of this script is to establish, regularly refresh, and support efforts to strengthen the foundations of life!

-:oOo:-